THE WEDDING
SURPRISE

THE WEDDING SURPRISE

BY

TRISH WYLIE

MILLS & BOON®

First published in Great Britain 2005
Large Print edition 2006
Harlequin Mills & Boon Limited,
Eton House, 18-24 Paradise Road,
Richmond, Surrey TW9 1SR

© Trish Wylie 2005

ISBN 0 263 18973 2

Set in Times Roman 16½ on 18½ pt.
16-0506-46756

Printed and bound in Great Britain
by Antony Rowe Ltd, Chippenham, Wiltshire

CHAPTER ONE

'How bad is it, Dad, really? I need to know.'

'There's no point in both of us worrying about it.'

'What happened to ''A problem shared''?'

'It still lives in the same region as ''What you don't know won't hurt you''.'

Caitlin Rourke blinked at her father's familiar face. He had gone grey in both complexion and hair colour over the last year, and it was worrying her.

She watched with suspicion as he smiled a smile that didn't quite make it all the way to his dark eyes. And she sighed in frustration.

'I know there's something seriously wrong.' She pulled up a chair in front of his ancient oak desk and sat down, leaning her elbows on the desk's edge and leaning forward to stare him in the eye. 'Maybe I can help.'

Echoing her sigh, Brendan Rourke leaned back in his leather chair and shook his head. 'Not this time.'

'You don't know that.' Her voice softened.

'Yes, baby, I do.'

'Well, maybe I'd like to know what's wrong before I decide for myself. You're the one who always told us to know all the facts and look at things from every angle before we made a decision.'

Brendan smiled softly as his words were used against him. 'It makes me feel old when my children use my own philosophies to win an argument.'

'You raised us all to question, to learn from all the things we do.' She grinned. 'You did a good job. You're one hell of a dad.'

His smile faded and he turned his eyes from hers, looking around his office walls. 'At least I can say I've done one thing right, then.'

Silence invaded the room as Caitlin searched his face again. She'd been noticing changes in him in the last few months when she'd visited. The normally confident manner in which he held himself had started to change first. There had been a slump to his broad shoulders. Then gradually he'd become more silent, introverted and brooding. And that just wasn't the man she knew and loved.

There was something wrong, and it was *big*.

'Tell me, Dad, or I'll live in this office 'til you do.' Her heart skipped a little as she asked the question that had been torturing her for weeks. 'Are you sick?'

His eyes shot to meet hers with a look of surprise. 'No, I'm not sick. Why would you think that?'

The fact that he'd lost so much weight. Something a man of his size just didn't carry well. The whole grey complexion thing…

'Is it Mum?'

Brendan frowned as he leaned forward, resting his elbows on the opposite side of the desk. 'Sweetheart, nobody is sick.'

She let a breath out. It had been her biggest worry. As people got older they were only too aware of the fact that they wouldn't have their parents for ever.

But if it wasn't that then there was only one thing it could be. 'It's the business, isn't it?'

He leaned back in his chair again. Studied her face for long seconds while she raised her eyebrows in question. Then eventually he nodded. 'Yes.'

'Well, then, we'll find a way to fix it together, all of us. It's what we do, remember?'

His eyes filled with sadness. 'This can't be fixed that easily. I've allowed this to happen through my own stupidity and there's nothing more I can do now.'

Caitlin's face transformed into a look of dogged determination her father knew only too well.

'If it's a money thing we'll find the money.'

'I already found the money. Three times now.' He sighed with resignation. 'And now it's not just the business we'll lose.'

'What else?'

'The house.'

Caitlin's breath caught. Not *home*. Not the one place in the world that could be relied upon for security and unquestioning love. It was a haven for all of them. A place filled with a million memories. They couldn't lose that after all this time. They just couldn't.

'What's gone wrong?'

'Cashflow. That's all. Downfall of many a business before this one, and I'm sure we won't be the last. People don't pay us, so I can't pay the people we need to pay. I borrowed until I had to remortgage, and now I can't borrow any more.'

His words circled around her head and took long moments to be absorbed into her brain. When eventually she'd grasped the severity of it all she blinked slowly as she asked the obvious. 'How much would it take to get us out of the hole?'

Brendan smiled a small, sad smile. 'More than you could get.'

'How much, Dad?'

Leaning back in his chair made the leather creak beneath him. The sound filled the silent room as he considered not telling her. But the determination in her eyes was unwavering. 'Seventy thousand.'

Caitlin's eyes widened. It was way more than she had in her own savings. Probably more than her brothers and sister could manage from their own savings. Hell, probably more than they all had combined.

She studied her father's face again. And she could see it. The defeat. The disappointment. The sense of failure. It broke her heart to see him that way. The strong bear of a man who had possessed enough love to solve a million smaller problems for his growing children. But not enough means to hold together the business he'd spent most of his life building.

Immediately her mind jumped to Aisling, the friend of a friend she'd spent most of yesterday evening on the phone with. Aisling had had a proposal to put to her. One that Caitlin had laughed about for hours.

Suddenly it didn't seem so ridiculous.

Now it was an escape route.

Nodding at the decision she'd silently made, she pushed the chair back from the desk and walked around to wrap her arms around her father's neck. 'We're going to get through this,

Dad. You wait and see. You're the one who taught us that we're stronger together than apart.'

The breath he took was shaky. 'There's no way out of this one, sweetheart.'

'Yes, there is. There's always a way. Everything happens for a reason.' She leaned back from him, her face barely inches from his, and smiled, 'No more secrets, Dad. That's what family is for. Someone wise told me that once.'

He nodded with a small smile at her words. 'All right. No more secrets.'

She kissed his forehead, her eyes closing. No more secrets. Apart from the massive one she was going to have to carry to get them out of this.

'God, I'm thrilled you're doing this.' Aisling hugged her tightly after she'd walked into the airy office. 'You're going to be just amazing.'

Pulling back from the embrace, Caitlin looked at her with narrow eyes. 'I don't know

about the amazing part, but I'm glad one of us
is thrilled.'

'It's an exciting project for all of us.'
Aisling moved back and sat down on the large
sofa that took up half of one wall in her office.
'It's taken eighteen months to set it running,
and I for one can't wait to get started.'

'Mmm.' Caitlin moved across to join her.
Taking a breath, she turned on the sofa, tuck-
ing one of her legs beneath the other. 'Can we
just go through it again?'

'You're not nervous?'

'Me?' She laughed. 'Nah. Hell, I always lie
to my family and friends for money from a TV
show.'

'You *are* nervous.' Aisling smiled a smile
that said *Trust me*. 'That's understandable. It's
nothing out of the ordinary. I'd be nervous
too.'

'You're not the one who'll be living a lie.'

'Why do you think I was so keen on it being
you?'

Caitlin raised an eyebrow at the question.
'Because as someone you already know I'm

less likely to sue you if it all goes pear-shaped?'

Aisling laughed at her reasoning. 'Well, that's one I hadn't thought of, but I guess I can tick that box now too.'

'I tick off boxes?'

'Tons of the things.' She started counting them out on her long fingers. 'You're single and unattached; you'll be sensational on camera; you have this amazingly close family and you have good reason to want the pay-off at the end.'

Dark eyes widened ever so slightly at the last 'tick'. 'What good reason, exactly?'

Aisling looked surprised she'd even asked. 'What a strange question.' She frowned. 'You do still want that restaurant of yours, don't you?'

It was all she'd wanted ever since she'd trained as a chef. Her own place to be creative in. But her priorities had changed now. There were other things, much more important, that needed the money.

Another lie wouldn't make much difference, though. 'Sure I do.'

'Well, then…'

'What about the guy?'

'Aiden?' Her face lit up, 'Oh, he's a blinder. We all just adore him. Wait 'til you meet him…'

Caitlin cringed at the thought. She didn't want to meet him. Ever. Given the choice.

If he was as unsuitable for her as Aisling thought he would be then she was going to hate every moment of being around him.

But that was the whole premise of Aisling's new show. Two completely different people pretending to be in love. All they had to do was persuade their families and friends that it was true. Then, to collect, they had to say their fake 'I do's with all of their family and friends present. Easy as pie, right?

Three months. Three months of living a lie with a camera crew following their every movement. But it would be worth every tor-turous moment of invasion of Caitlin's precious privacy if it saved her father's business and the magical place called *home*.

Caitlin's chin raised a notch. She could do this. She had to. Even while her stomach churned and her hands were clammy. It was only three months.

And, after all, how bad could this Aiden guy really be?

CHAPTER TWO

AIDEN FLYNN turned as the door opened and then stared at the woman who was now his 'fiancée' for the next few months.

She was stunning. Not a bit of wonder they'd chosen her from all the candidates suggested. He'd bet she'd look great on screen. A hell of a lot better than he was looking anyway. But six months in front of a computer, within arm's reach of billions of calories, hadn't exactly helped any.

And he could tell she wasn't impressed. When she'd opened the door she'd been smiling openly. But now, as her eyes moved over him, he could see that smile fading in her dark eyes.

Suddenly he wished he'd bothered to remove the abnormal amount of hair on his face. That he'd taken maybe ten minutes to visit a barber in the last week. But Aisling had been fairly adamant that he stayed the way he was. He was perfect the way he was, she'd said.

Shame that Caitlin Rourke didn't think so. Because she really was stunning.

His eyes moved down from the urchin cut of her rich brown hair, over flawless creamy skin to the sensual bow of her mouth. Then they dared to move further, down over her long neck to the curve of her small breasts and the inward sweep of her slender waist. Oh, yeah. She was something. And way out of his usual league if the designer cut of her clothes and the swanky place she lived in were anything to go by.

His eyes moved back up as she smoothed her short hair behind one ear and smiled at him again before moving forward.

She then stunned him completely by throwing her arms around his neck and pressing her slender body tightly against his. Blinking in confusion, he wrapped his arms around her waist with jerky movements.

'You're here at last!' She tilted her head back to look up at him. 'I've missed you so much.'

Aiden's eyes widened. 'Well, I've missed you too.'

Her eyes jerked to her left and he followed the movement until his own found the camera pointing at him. Aha. Straight to business, then…

She leaned in to kiss his cheek above the line of his beard, leaving her cheek there and whispering, 'My sister is here.' Then she leaned back again to look at him.

Tightening his arms around her waist to signal he understood, he then did what any self-respecting fiancé would do and leaned down for a kiss. After all, her sister would expect it…

Caitlin's eyes widened as the realisation of his intention hit her. She ducked her head further back and laughed slightly. 'Oh, no, you don't. Not with that beard.'

She thought he'd grown that beard overnight? If they'd only recently got engaged then she'd have been kissing him with that beard for some time now.

'You didn't complain about where this beard went last weekend, honey.'

A dark eyebrow quirked at his response and a spark entered her eyes. A challenge? he wondered.

Her voice came out like warm honey. 'You have no idea the places I ended up with beard rash.'

A challenge indeed.

His eyes sparkled back at her. 'Maybe you should show me later.'

'We'll have to see about that.' And as quickly as that the spark was gone from her eyes and she pulled back from his embrace. She glanced towards the living room, then her eyes flickered back to meet his as her voice dropped. 'That beard has to go.'

'We're not even married yet and already you're trying to change me?'

She looked him over with a cursory glance, taking stock of the raw material the show had given her. Then with a small smile she nodded. 'Hell, yes.'

*   *   *

The sister stared at him with a similar look of surprise as he entered the warm-coloured room. Aiden was sensing a pattern here. What was it? Had he two heads? All right, so right that second he might not look like a pin-up, but he wasn't exactly serial killer material either. At least he didn't think he was.

'Hi.'

Caitlin watched her sister blink at him a couple of times before she stared back at her with wide eyes. The news of her 'engagement' not five minutes earlier hadn't exactly gone too well. And the fact that she'd had to explain the presence of TV cameras in her life in an earlier phone call only added to the lack of reality. She was in the Twilight Zone. Something her sister had pointed out only seconds before Aiden's arrival.

'This is Aiden.'

'The internet guy?'

She smiled as she followed the story they'd been given. 'Yes, this is him.'

'The guy you're getting married to?'

'Yes.'

She opened her mouth to make a comment. Then her eyes moved to the camera at the end of the room and she pinned a smile on her mouth as she rose from the large sofa. 'It's nice to meet you, Aiden. I'm Cara.'

Aiden hadn't missed the hesitation before she stood to offer her hand to him. There'd been a comment coming there, he'd just bet. 'It's nice to finally meet you. I've heard a lot about you.'

The smile stayed in place as she shook his hand. 'More than I've heard about you, I'm sure. You're quite a surprise.'

He laughed as he released her hand. 'I'd say so.'

Cara continued to stare at him. It was like being a bug under a microscope. He stepped closer to Caitlin and grinned. 'Well, honey, I'll just throw my bag upstairs.'

'Good plan.' She reversed a few steps towards the door.

'No, it's all right. I know where I'm going.' The lie flowed smoothly from his mouth. 'You stay here and chat to Cara. I'll be right back.'

Both women stood stock still, smiles in place, as he moved past Caitlin to leave the room. With a smile back at her sister he then reached out a hand and pinched Caitlin's rear on his way out.

'Are you out of your mind?'

He heard Cara's whispered words as he walked upstairs. It had been a long time since he'd made such a lasting impression on two women.

Catching sight of himself in a large mirror as he reached the top of the flight of stairs, he smiled wryly. He guessed he couldn't blame them. He looked like hell.

He stared at his own eyes in the reflection. They were the only part of himself he still recognised.

Everything else had pretty much gone to pot. His dark hair stuck out in varying curls where it reached the collar of his favourite old checked shirt. His hair was longer than he'd worn it since his university days. And as for the hair on his face. Well, Caitlin was right. It had to go. He looked as if he'd just walked off a desert island.

His dark eyebrows quirked up under his long fringe as he realised that technically he might as well have.

He'd spent the last six months in solitude, with only a ghost for company. And work. His own work and the ghost's work. It had been fairly surreal.

Moving away from the mirror and along the softly lit hall, he found himself looking at frame upon frame of photographs. Caitlin Rourke's life laid out before him. Pictures of her laughing, smiling at the people around her with love in her eyes. Close-ups of her curled up on a sofa, caught off guard as she looked up into the camera lens. Shots of an autumn day when she'd had longer hair tossed by an unseen wind. Every one showed scenes of a happy, contented woman, in love with life and living.

Caitlin Rourke was everything he wasn't. And a familiar ache, so old it burned like a physical pain in the pit of his stomach, made him unexpectedly angry with her for that.

'Are you out of your mind?'

Still reeling from the fact that her new fiancé had just pinched her behind, Caitlin blinked at her sister. 'What?'

'What are you doing?' Cara glanced at the invasive camera beside them, turned her back on it and whispered, 'You're planning on marrying *him*?'

It didn't take much searching to see the disapproval on her sister's face. With a deep breath Caitlin prepared to take the steps to weave her lie. 'You don't know him like I do.'

A burst of sarcastic laughter hit the air. 'Obviously not. Because whatever it is about him is hidden under about twenty feet of hair.'

Which would be gone by the morning if Caitlin had her way. She couldn't abide men with facial hair. As a child they'd had an uncle with a beard who had made her cry every time she was asked to kiss him goodbye.

'You just need time to get to know him, Cara.'

'Like you have?' Cara shook her head. 'This is just too weird, Caitlin. How can you possibly know this man well enough to want to marry him?'

'We've been talking for months.'

'On the internet?'

'Yes. On the internet.'

'And you know him well enough from that to spend the rest of your life with him?'

'Yes.' The lies came almost too easily, 'And you can't know him well enough in two minutes to make a judgement on him.'

Cara stared at her for what felt like for ever but was probably only a minute. Then she shook her head. 'This isn't like you, Cait. He's not like anyone you've ever dated, and all this camera stuff is mad.'

Caitlin sighed. 'I told you—it's just a programme about people who've found love over the internet.'

'And you're telling me that every time any of us talk with you it's all going to be filmed?'

'It's just a few months and then they'll be gone.'

'Well...' She glanced over her shoulder at the camera again. 'With any luck it won't be the only thing that's gone.'

Caitlin reached a hand out and squeezed her sister's arm. 'Give him a chance, Cara. He can't be that bad.' She frowned at her mistake. Surely she would know herself that he wasn't that bad if she was marrying him? 'He's a great guy. At least I think he is. Just give it some time.'

Eyes as dark as her own stared at her before Cara sighed. 'I think I'm more hurt that you didn't tell me before now. We always talk about everything. This is the first time we haven't.'

Caitlin's throat threatened to close at the words that were only too true.

'It just feels like something has changed with you and me.' Cara's voice broke slightly, betraying her emotions. 'And I hate that.'

Caitlin blinked back tears as Cara pulled her into a hug before turning to leave, with an 'I'll talk to you tomorrow' thrown over her shoulder.

'This sucks already.' She glanced into the camera, 'You have no idea.'

She frowned down at the carpet, then glanced up at the ceiling. It was time to go and meet her fiancé. With a silent plea to the overhead light that a book really couldn't be judged by its cover, she turned on her heel to go upstairs.

CHAPTER THREE

BY THE time Caitlin reached the hallway he was halfway down the stairs. She tilted her head back and looked up at him, her eyes meeting his. They were the one feature she could see that she liked. So blue they belonged on a movie screen, and they seemed to spark back at her. Surely someone with eyes as blue as a summer's sky couldn't be all that bad?

'Hey.'

She blinked up at him. 'Hey.'

'So you're my fiancée, then?'

She smiled at the statement. 'So it would appear.'

He nodded and his eyes sparkled with amusement. 'Big hit with your sister, wasn't I?'

Caitlin quirked a dark brow beneath the annoying fringe that kept on falling in her eye.

'Mmm, well, she's a bit protective. You're in for a lot of that, I'm afraid.'

Shoving large hands into the pockets of his faded jeans, Aiden studied her before asking, 'Your family is close?'

Caitlin nodded. 'Yes.'

'Then this can't be an easy thing for you to do.'

She suddenly felt vulnerable as he studied her, her head beginning to pound at the temples. She'd never been with someone who could make the very air around them feel oppressive to her. It wasn't a nice sensation. Particularly not in her own home.

'And lying comes naturally to you, I suppose?'

Aiden merely shrugged at the question. 'I've done it from time to time, growing up. When it was called for.'

Her fringe fell back out of her eye as she tilted her head and studied him. This stranger. How could anyone with eyes so warm be so cold? And how would she ever know a word he said to her was true if he was so open about lying?

A sudden burst of male laughter caught her off guard.

'That shocks you, does it?'

'I don't know if shock is the word I would have used. It surprises me that you're so open about it, I guess.' She smiled a small smile. 'But maybe that's what they had in mind when they chose you. An experienced liar might be able to teach me the ropes.'

He continued smiling. 'Could be. But they certainly got the opposites thing right.'

Her eyes moved over him again as she nodded in agreement. 'Yes, so it would appear.'

He removed his hands and started slowly down towards her. Each step seemed measured, controlled. And when he stood on the step above her he leaned his face closer to hers to ask in a low voice, 'So, how do we make them all believe we're in love, Caitlin Rourke?'

She swallowed hard as she looked into his eyes close up. They were really stunning. And another sense awoke to discover he actually smelled extremely good. She took a deep breath and found the scent almost calming. Reassuring in its maleness. He was just some guy, after all.

She tilted her chin slightly upwards. 'I guess it might be an idea to try getting to know each other better.'

Aiden quirked a brow at her. 'And how do you suggest we do that?'

'Talking would be the traditional route. And we're supposed to have been doing months of that on the internet.' She thought for a moment, trying to get her brain around the problem. 'Or we could make out a set of questions for each other and write it all out.'

'Like a study guide?'

'Exactly!' She smiled at his understanding. 'That makes perfect sense.'

Aiden watched as her face was transformed with enthusiasm. Her dark eyes sparkled and she smiled more openly at him. Hell, what was she? Alice in Wonderland, or something? She had the same enthusiasm levels as a ten-year-old. 'Keep your panties on, honey, it's only a handful of questions. It's not an unbreakable guide to cashing the big cheque.'

The smile disappeared. 'You really are very rude, aren't you?'

'Because I mentioned your underwear or because I just rained on your parade?'

Her hands planted themselves firmly on her hips as she glared up at him. 'Just because I happen to get enthusiastic about the fact that we might actually manage to do something pro-active about this it means you should shoot me down, does it? Why are you even doing this show if you have no intention of us winning at the end?'

'Oh, I have every intention of winning at the end. And I'm all for anything that achieves that.'

'So the idea of doing some work towards that would be a bad idea because...?'

'I didn't say it was a bad idea.'

She was flabbergasted. 'But you just said—'

Aiden smiled calmly below his beard. 'I just said you shouldn't get so thrilled at the prospect of having to swot up on each other. It's not exactly riveting stuff, learning what toothpaste we each use.'

Caitlin rocked back on her heels. She had never met anyone like Aiden before. How on earth were they supposed to get on well enough to fool everyone if they couldn't even hold a simple conversation?

He watched the varying emotions play across her face and continued smiling his secret smile. She didn't get him at all. And he quite liked that. It made him feel he was in control. Something to knock her neat little world out of joint. That would be one way of punishing her for having such a damned perfect life.

'You really are something out of a 1950s TV show, aren't you?'

Caitlin blinked up in the dim light at the voice that sounded from across her hall. It made sense that they should spend some time in her house playing the 'getting to know each other' game. But when she'd agreed she hadn't realised she was going to be stuck under the same roof with someone so damned annoying.

They'd made out a set of questions for each other, swapped them to fill in the answers, and had then retreated to different parts of the house to 'study up'. After four hours of learning how many sugars he took in his coffee and what side of the bed he slept on her head had gone numb, so she'd opted for fleecy pyjamas and the security of her huge bed.

But with the door to her room slightly ajar she could still see the light shining from where Aiden lay in bed across the hall from her. She was only too aware of where he was in the house at any given time. Aware of the sounds of another human being sharing her space. But there wasn't the same comfort associated with those noises as there would have been if it were a friend or a family member staying.

She sighed into the air. 'What does that mean, exactly?'

'Everything in your life is just so bloody neat and pretty.'

'I happen to like a tidy house.' And she wasn't normally in it much, which helped. But she didn't mention that.

'I don't mean just your house.'

She rolled over to face the door, moving the pillow to fit underneath her neck better. 'So what *do* you mean?'

'I mean your whole life. Neat little family, neat crowd of friends, neat career direction. Your life is all wrapped up with ribbons and bows.'

Caitlin wished.

'You have no idea what my life is like.'

'That's what I'm in here studying.'

'You don't get a picture of someone's life from a set of questions dealing with what size feet they have or their favourite colour.'

There was silence for a few moments, and then Caitlin heard his bed creak slightly as he moved. 'So tell me something that's not on the questionnaire.'

'Like what?'

'Something that only someone you love would know.'

She pursed her lips and frowned at his words. He was looking for personal information. Something that meant she would have to give something of herself to him. And she really didn't want to do that. Didn't want this person she didn't like much knowing things he would still know when he walked away in three months.

Aiden strained to hear any movement when she didn't reply, holding his breath to keep silent.

'Caitlin?'

'I'm still here.'

He smiled at her small voice. She didn't want to tell him anything, did she?

'What's wrong? Skeletons in your closet?'

'Only ones wrapped neatly in ribbons and bows.'

Her sarcastic answer brought a larger smile to his face. 'Come on. One thing. I promise to forget it when the show ends.'

She turned her face into her pillow to call him a name, then came out to take a deep breath. 'We'll swap. You get one subject; I get to ask about one in return.'

He considered the proposal for a moment and then quirked a brow at the doorway. What harm could it do?

'Okay.'

Caitlin waited. Then waited some more. 'So?'

'I'm thinking.'

'Don't strain yourself.'

'Funny.' He propped himself up on an elbow and continued to stare at the door, as if by staring harder he would be able to see through it to read her face. 'So how come there's no neat boyfriend around to complete the picture?'

Damn. He just *would* ask that, wouldn't he?

'Maybe I like being single.'

'You're twenty-eight years old. In the fifties you'd be a spinster already. Don't you want neat little kids so you can scrub their little faces and read them fairy stories at night?'

'That's a second question.'

'Oops.'

She raised herself up on an elbow and thought about her answer. To tell or not to tell. That was the question, really.

'I used to have a boyfriend. A fiancé.'

He wasn't surprised at the first part of her answer, but the second part caught him off guard. 'What happened?'

She took a breath. 'He died.'

Aiden flumped onto his back and frowned at the ceiling. 'How?'

'He had this stupid motorcycle that he loved nearly as much as he said he loved me.'

'Was it long ago?'

Yesterday, she wanted to answer. There were still odd moments when it felt as if it was. But the moments were further apart now than they had been at the start. The pain she'd felt back then was a bearable numbness now.

'Nearly five years. We met in high school.'

Aiden heard the matter-of-fact tone of her voice as she recited facts that must have hurt like hell at the time. Her perfect life had hit a glitch. A big one. And that made him think. 'I'm sorry.'

Caitlin was surprised by the softness in his voice. It was a completely different tone for the sarcastic edge he'd had with her for most of the evening. She sank back down into the haven of her duvet and lifted the bottom of it with her legs to tuck her feet in. Those two words spoken with that softness making her reach out for a simpler form of comfort, she supposed.

She blinked upwards for several long seconds, then replied with an equally softly spoken, 'Thanks.'

The house fell silent again, until Caitlin's voice sounded out with, 'So, no neat little girlfriend for you, then?'

He laughed. 'No, nothing neat in my life.'

'You're this charming to everyone, then?'

'Careful, Caitlin. I'll get the impression you don't like me much.'

'Oh, and that would hurt your feelings, would it?'

'Well, if you still think I have feelings then I'm not a lost cause just yet, am I?'

She smiled. 'Every human being has to have a feeling on something or another. I'll allow you that much.'

'Cheers.' He turned his head to smile back at the door.

'You're welcome.'

Aiden was surprised when it went silent again. She was quitting that easily? He was almost disappointed that she was. Not that he was up for a deep psychoanalysis of his own life. But she had told him something very personal, had allowed something painful to be talked about, even briefly. And he felt he owed her something back for that.

'Six months.'

'What?'

'Six months. It's how long I can manage to stay in a relationship with a woman, apparently.'

Caitlin thought about the unexpectedly volunteered information. 'How come?'

'I wear them out.'

She laughed at his joke. 'I'll bet.'

He smiled. 'I guess I'm just not neat little marriage material.'

'No kids to scrub and read fairy stories to, huh?'

The ache in his stomach came back. 'I don't have any experience on either of those things.'

She turned her head towards the door at his answer. 'Your mother didn't scrub your face and read you fairy tales when you were little?'

None of them had. They'd had so many kids in their care that it had been miraculous enough if they all made it through each day fed and watered. Fairy tales hadn't exactly been on the menu at any stage.

'That's a second question.'

She opened her mouth to push him on it, but he got there first. 'That's probably enough to add to the lists—for one night anyway.' The bed creaked again as he turned away from the door and switched off the bedside light. 'Goodnight, Caitlin Rourke.'

Caitlin blinked into the darkness, her eyes adjusting to make out the dark forms of her bedroom furniture while her mind worked overtime. Aiden had more facets than he first appeared to have. And that intrigued her.

The fact that it intrigued her bothered her.

She'd never met anyone like him before. But the simple fact was in three months' time she'd probably never meet him again.

'Goodnight, Aiden.'

CHAPTER FOUR

THE fixed cameras in her house were replaced by a camera guy and a sound man during the day. And by lunchtime Caitlin knew more about them both than she knew about her 'fiancé'.

They just had an openness that she was more accustomed to. In conversation they shared information that might have been simple in its general topic but gave hints to their personalities and lives. Whereas Aiden just had a way of avoiding anything remotely like sharing. He could be an international spy for all she knew.

Except for that brief time that they'd shared talking from separate rooms across the hallway.

She struggled her way through the lunchtime rush at Maguires, the employer of her choice in Dublin city centre. The dream of having a restaurant of her own was so far off that it made sense to work somewhere she at least liked to fill the time. But with Aiden Flynn, international man of mystery, sitting at home in her house it was hard to concentrate on dish presentation.

Faking a headache, she left the restaurant and piled into her car with Mick and Joe to make the drive home.

'So you're taking Aiden home to meet your parents tomorrow, then?' Mick pointed the camera at her from the passenger seat.

'Mmm.' She grimaced slightly at the thought. 'That's the plan.'

'You worried about it?'

'Oh, no. We tell massive porkies to each other all the time. It's a sort of family hobby of ours.'

Mick laughed. 'Mine too.'

She risked a massive insurance claim by glancing into the lens for a second, 'I was kidding, Mick.'

'Oh, me too.'

She laughed. 'Seriously. My family is close. Really close.' Her expression changed. 'After Liam died they were there to hold me together. On the days when I couldn't get up they brought me food in bed. When I couldn't stay still my father even took up jogging to keep me company.'

Glancing back at the camera, she smiled sadly. 'Where one of us ends the other begins. It's just the way we are.'

'That's a rare thing, all right.'

'Yes, it is.'

She wove her way through the traffic, her mind focussing on the task of not hitting another vehicle. But as they got out of the city and headed towards the suburbs her mind went back to a darker time than the sunny autumn day they were currently in.

'Do you still miss him, Caitlin?'

The softly voiced question caught her off guard. It had been a long time since anyone had asked. She thought about it a while, played snapshots of memories across her mind, and smiled wistfully as she answered. 'I miss the sound of his voice sometimes.'

The sound of the camera filled the silence.

'You tend to think that someone the same age as you will just always be around. Especially when it's someone you love.' She continued smiling, eyes on the road ahead but her mind reliving he past. 'Liam was always the one who lived for the moment. He used to say life was too short to just stand still.'

She glanced at the camera again. 'Maybe he knew.'

She made the turn into her street and parked in front of her house. Switching off the engine, she glanced up at the windows. Was he looking out at her, Aiden Flynn man of mystery?

'Aiden's different from Liam?'

The question raised a small laugh. 'Like night and day.'

'Aiden?'

'In the kitchen—and aren't you supposed to yell ''Hi, honey, I'm home''?'

She smiled as she walked through the living room to the open kitchen/dining room. 'I'll remember next time.' Her eyes roved over the mess on her normally immaculate kitchen surfaces. 'What are you doing?'

He quirked an eyebrow at the question. 'I was hungry.'

'So you thought it would be an idea to massacre my kitchen?'

'It would have been perfect when you got home.' He pointed an accusatory finger at her. 'You're early.'

She watched as he nodded at her crew.

'I told them I had a headache.'

Concern crossed his eyes. 'You're sick?'

Caitlin's eyes focussed on the spoon suspended in mid-air as he stared at her. In slow motion drips of red something dripped onto her cooker. 'No.'

'Getting quite good at this lying thing, aren't we?'

'I don't think that actually counts as a lie.' She continued watching the dripping. A small pool formed on the surface. Whatever it was, it had better wash off.

'I guess it's all about degrees of lying.' He watched her face as he thought out loud. 'What constitutes a big lie and what's a fib.'

'A fib, in theory, doesn't hurt people. It may even save their feelings, depending on the situation.' Her eyes searched for the nearest cloth. 'What *is* that stuff you're dripping all over the place?'

Aiden waved the spoon as he looked at it. 'I'm making cheese on beans on toast.'

Her eyes moved up to lock with his. 'You're making *what*?'

'Cheese on beans on toast.' He grinned, white teeth peeking out from the shroud of his beard. 'C'mon—you haven't heard of it? And you call yourself a chef?'

'I cook food that tastes good.'

'This tastes good—' He waved the spoon again and small splatters of red appeared on his white T-shirt. 'Believe me.'

Frowning at the modern art piece her cooker was rapidly becoming, she retorted with, 'I'm quite sure the air in my mouth tastes better than that.'

'Well, I wouldn't know that, would I? What with you refusing to kiss me and all…'

Caitlin refused to rise to the bait. 'That had better get washed off before it becomes glue.'

Aiden glanced at the camera between them and winked, then studied the telltale flush that touched Caitlin's cheeks. 'You know you're going to have to do it at some stage.'

'You made the mess; you clean it.'

'I wasn't referring to the mess.'

'I was.' Her chin rose as she stared him straight in the eye.

Aiden stared right back. 'It has to happen for all this to be convincing.'

An eyebrow quirked. 'Next you'll be suggesting we sleep together for the sake of realism. I didn't sign up for that kind of a show.'

The male hormones in his body transmitted a very vivid mental image from her words, and Aiden frowned. Six months alone had made him a raging sex maniac all of a sudden?

'Honey, you'd better watch that head of yours doesn't get too large for the doorways in this place.'

'I am not kissing you while that beard is there, so you can forget it!'

'You're prejudiced against beards for some reason?'

'As a matter of fact, I am.'

'Because…?'

He waited patiently for an explanation, filling the time by stirring the bubbling beans in the saucepan in front of him.

When there was no explanation volunteered he glanced at her from the corner of his eye. 'Well?'

Caitlin was annoyed by how easily he made her angry. She was usually cool, calm and collected. Occupational necessities when restaurants were full and head chefs were yelling in hot kitchens. But Aiden could raise a spark in her from a glance, a single statement—from several spots of tomatoey sauce on her cookertop.

'Well, what?'

He removed the pan from the hob and said nothing.

Caitlin sighed in frustration. 'They scratch.'

He hid a smile as he removed toast from the grill and laid it on two plates.

'And they do actually cause rashes on sensitive skin.'

Another mental picture formed. 'You never did get round to showing me that.'

Her mouth quirked at the edges. 'And neither will I.'

'Spoilsport.'

The quirk became a smile as she moved closer to watch his attempt at arranging cheese on beans on toast to make it look appetising. When she was right by his shoulder she lowered her voice and asked, 'Aiden Flynn, are you flirting with me?'

Aiden continued concentrating on his masterpiece. 'Is it working?'

She leaned in close to his ear to whisper, 'No.'

He smiled as he sprinkled the last of the grated cheese. 'Well, then obviously I'm not.'

Lifting a plate, he turned to wave it beneath her nose while looking into her eyes. 'Because if I *was* flirting with you it *would* be working.'

Caitlin's dark eyes studied his too blue eyes just inches from hers. She searched for answers, for the reasons behind his Jekyll and Hyde personality. But all she could see looking back at her was a warm sparkle of challenge. As if it was some kind of game to him. Maybe it was. Maybe his way of coping with the next few months was to make it 'fun'. He obviously hadn't as much to lose as she did if it didn't work.

'I need this thing to work, Aiden.'

He blinked long dark lashes at her with a question in his eyes. 'The show?'

'Yes.'

'Why is it so important?'

She avoided his questioning eyes with a downward glance at the plate. 'It just is.'

Aiden had read her questionnaire for the show and memorised over and over the study guide from the night before. 'You want your own restaurant that badly?'

'As badly as you want to fund whatever it is you need a year off work for.'

He continued to hold a steady gaze as she looked back into his eyes. It was what he'd filled in on his own questionnaire. And it was half true, in a way. He needed what the show would bring him to take time to fulfil a promise. To complete a legacy. On the form all he'd said was 'to fund a career break'. But the words didn't even cover half of the story.

The look in her eyes said she wanted to know more.

Aiden wasn't ready for even half an answer. 'It's important to me too.'

She seemed to think about pushing him for an explanation, but with a shrug of her shoulders she let it go. 'Then we're together on this?'

'I guess we are.'

A small nod, and then she reached out to take the plate from him. 'Then maybe you should stop making this into a game of some kind.'

'That's my doing, is it?'

'Isn't it? All this word-play you have us doing?'

'A game is exactly what this thing is. Why shouldn't it be fun along the way?'

Because there was too much to lose.

Avoiding his *ridiculously* blue eyes, she turned and took her plate to the table over-looking the small outdoor courtyard. 'For us both to win we need to work together. To con-centrate on what we're doing. With no distrac-tions. And we can't do that if you keep playing with words and taunting me.'

'Oh, I see.' He picked up his own plate and moved across to join her. 'We should run it like some kind of military campaign, should we? Every word and gesture rehearsed ahead of time?'

'Yes.' She frowned at him as he sat down and handed her a knife and fork. 'We have to plan for every eventuality.'

He thought about her words for a few mo-ments, then asked in a calm voice, 'Is that how you run your life? Everything planned out in advance?'

'It makes sense.' She continued frowning at him. His lack of approval was evident. 'You set yourself goals, targets to aim for, and you work 'til you get there. I suppose that's very alien to you and your bohemian approach to a career?'

'You can't plan for everything. No matter how you try to. That's life.' He spooned a forkful of food into his mouth, chewed a couple of times, and continued talking with his mouth full. 'You should know that from what happened to your fiancé.'

His words were like a blow to her chest and she felt her eyes stinging angrily. 'How dare you?'

Pushing her chair back from the table, she glared down at him from above. 'How dare you throw that at me like it was some little glitch in my great plan for life? Some little wobble that I should have planned for!'

He swallowed his food, looking up at her with a frown, 'That's not what I meant.'

'That's exactly what you meant. You're trying to prove that your way of living life, from one opportunity to the next without any ties or emotional involvement, is a better way of living.'

He remained calm. 'That's not what I said.'

Caitlin flung an arm in the air at her side. 'You who has never had a relationship that lasted more than sixty seconds!'

'Six months.'

She ignored him and leaned down to press home her words. 'At least I *had* love in my life, Aiden. Even if it was taken from me before either of us had planned.' She tilted her head to one side and stared at him with sparkling eyes. 'And I wouldn't trade a single second of it. Is there anything in your life you can honestly say the same thing about?'

Without waiting for an answer she spun on her heel and left the room at speed, before running up to her room and slamming the door.

CHAPTER FIVE

AIDEN listened to her running footsteps up the stairs and along the landing, and heard the slam of her door. Then he took a deep breath and leaned back in his chair.

Well, hell.

There was movement from his side and Mick turned the camera on him for a close-up.

'Go away, Mick.' Aiden didn't even look at him as he spoke the words. 'Give me a second, here.'

'No can do. My boss would kill me.'

'Your boss will thump you if you don't.' He glanced up at the lens. 'And you *know* I pack a mean punch.'

Mick grinned behind the camera. 'Touchy today, aren't we?'

'Mick—'

The glare would have been enough to make most grown men step back at least a couple of steps. But Mick merely continued grinning. 'It's in my contract to film everything. Them's the rules.'

'I *wrote* the damn rules.'

'Well, you dug yourself a bit of a hole there, then, didn't you?'

With a shake of his head he looked past Mick's shoulder to the courtyard beyond. 'Remind me never to hire you again.'

The camera continued rolling as Aiden stared off into space. Then, after several minutes' silence, Mick spoke with a soft voice. 'Finding this one tough, huh?'

He smiled a small smile. 'She's not what I expected, I guess.'

It was an interesting dilemma. He thought back over the brief he'd originally put together for the show and the plan he'd formulated from it. He'd had a type of woman in mind from the start, but Caitlin Rourke was a surprise to him. She was—*more* than he'd expected.

'More complicated.'

'You expected some party girl who would see this all as some big fun game?'

'Maybe I did.'

There was a second's pause. 'A bit like Caitlin just said, in a way.'

After another brief glare Aiden closed his eyes and sighed. 'Probably.'

'But it's not a game to her.'

'Yeah.' He opened his eyes and smiled sarcastically. 'Because owning a fancy place of her own is such a big deal.'

'And that's wrong in your eyes?' Mick frowned slightly as he asked the question. 'Is it wrong for her to get that because she's so young, or something?'

'Things that matter that much are sweeter when you work hard for them. When you've had to make sacrifices along the way. It makes it more worthwhile when you achieve your goals.'

'More honourable than lying your way there? Or fooling the people that you care about along the way?'

'I happen to think so.'

The camera continued rolling.

'She's had an easy go of it up 'til now. Everything all neat and tidy.'

'Apart from Liam.'

Aiden looked up at the lens again. 'Was that his name?'

Mick nodded without moving the camera an inch.

Aiden mirrored the nod. 'That had to hurt.' He looked up at the ceiling. 'Still does, by the looks of things.'

Hell.

With a frown he pushed his chair back from the table. Standing up, he looked at the camera again. 'I don't suppose I can persuade you two to stay here while I go grovel?'

Two heads shook in unison.

'Caitlin?'

There was silence from the other side of the closed door.

Aiden glanced at Mick and Joe, who both stared back at him.

'Look, I didn't mean to upset you about your fiancé. That wasn't what I was aiming for.'

The silence continued, and another sideways glance saw Mick shrug his shoulders and Joe smile weakly.

Then a small voice sounded from behind the pine door. 'What exactly *were* you aiming for, then?'

He thought his answer over carefully before stepping closer to the door. 'I was just trying to point out that you can't plan for everything. Neither of us can.'

The answering silence was deafening.

Aiden leaned his forehead against the door as he tried to think of something to say that wouldn't put both his size tens right in it again.

'I just don't know how else to get through this if we don't plan it out. My family knows me too well.'

The restaurant obviously meant more to her than he could possibly understand. In a small part of his mind he wanted her to have the guts to get it by herself. To fight and work for what she wanted rather than having it handed to her in some get-rich-quick scheme. He knew only too well from recent experience that she had enough backbone to stand up and fight against him when she believed he was out of line.

So where was that mettle when it came to fighting for her dream? It didn't make any sense.

But he had opened an old wound and he felt guilty about that. The best way to get rid of that ugly feeling would be to try and make amends.

'Tell me how you were with him.'

The bed creaked a little, and he could imagine her turning to look at the door.

'With Liam?'

'Yes, with Liam.' He leaned back from the door again and waited, his breath held still inside his chest.

'We flirted a lot.'

Aiden smiled and let the air escape in a small burst of laughter. 'You don't like it when *I* flirt with you.'

'You said you weren't flirting.'

Turning around, he grimaced slightly at the camera and then sat down on the floor with his back against the door. 'I may have lied about that. I did say I could lie when the cause arose.'

'Why would you do that?'

'Lie to you or flirt with you?'

'The second one.'

He leaned his head back. 'Maybe I'm just a flirtatious kinda guy.'

Her smile came through in her voice. 'Nah, not you. You're too sullen for that game.'

'You think I'm sullen?' A glance at his crew found them both smiling. 'All right, I guess I can be—a *little*. But maybe you bring out the flirty side of my nature.'

'You don't even *like* me, Aiden.'

It wasn't that he didn't like her. That was one of the things that probably bugged him the most. Having spent all morning alone in her house, he'd done a bit of an investigation and found everything from photograph albums to family videos. He liked what he'd seen just fine. *That* wasn't the problem.

'I think I'm maybe a little envious of you…' The words made their way out into the big wide world of their own accord. 'Of all people like you.'

She went silent again for a brief moment, then, 'Why?'

'Because not everyone's had this fairy tale of a life that you've had.'

'Losing Liam was hardly the best thing that ever happened to me.'

'I know.' He softened his voice. 'And I know that's something you'll probably never completely get over. But you were right in what you said. You were lucky to have found it in the first place. That doesn't happen to many people these days.'

When silence followed his words again he let the words keep coming. 'And you have a great family—a close family who are all there for you. It's why the show chose you. To see if you could manage to make all the people that know you so well believe in a lie.'

'And why did they choose you?'

They hadn't. He'd chosen himself. Because the role he had to play was so complex and only someone who had produced the thing from the very beginning could know what to do when things got difficult. To get the dramatic result they wanted. To make things difficult for Caitlin.

But in volunteering he'd also managed to fulfil another major criteria. He was as opposite to Caitlin Rourke as it was possible to be. In practically every way.

'Because I'm the flipside of you.'

'In what way?' There was barely a heartbeat of a pause before she figured it out. 'You don't have a family, do you?'

He frowned hard.

'None at all?'

The pity in her voice made him sick.

'Aiden?'

'What are you going to do about it, Caitlin? *Adopt me?* I'm a little past the age for you to do that.'

The bed creaked again and her voice sounded a little closer to the door. 'That's why you have no experience of fairy stories and your face being scrubbed?'

'Don't go crying on me in there.' He turned his head towards the door a little. 'There are millions of us around the world who didn't have a family of their own. I was one of the lucky ones. I had loads of families.'

'That's why you spend you life drifting around. No serious relationships, no long-term career. Because you have no grounding in those things.'

Actually, she was wrong on that one. He had a career. A damned good one, as it happened. He'd worked hard to get to the top of his game and he was hell on legs at it. But he couldn't tell her that or he'd blow the whole thing.

'I've been in serious relationships—'

'Serious relationships last longer than six months.'

'Not if they don't work out, they don't. Just because they're short doesn't mean they weren't great. That's life.'

'And why didn't they work out?'

He vaguely noticed that her voice sounded very close as he answered, 'They just didn't.'

There was a sliding noise against the door as Caitlin sat down on the opposite side of their protective barrier. 'What were you like with them?'

'Flirtatious, sullen, jealous, happy. More of everything. More alive. The usual share of things in any good relationship.'

They sat in a silent understanding after he spoke.

Aiden closed his eyes again for a few moments. Stunned by how much of himself he was giving to her in such a short space of time. He knew that reality shows often brought out an unusual level of intensity in people's relationships. But he really hadn't been prepared for it happening to *him*. It surprised him. But what surprised him more was that it didn't feel as if he'd just had teeth pulled. It felt somehow right. As if by being honest he had lifted some kind of barricade that he hadn't even known he'd been carrying around.

It was just weird that it was with someone like Caitlin.

Her voice was low, so quiet that he might not have heard it if he hadn't been a mere door's width away from her. 'Then that's how you need to be with me.'

'And how *you* were with Liam is how you need to be with me.'

'So that we can fool everyone into believing we're in love?'

'Yes.'

Her voice sounded different to his ears— uncertain, a little nervous. She was going out on a limb. Veering from her habit of a lifetime that had things all laid out and every eventuality prepared for. It was a big step for her, and Aiden knew that as soon as the words left her lips.

'Then that's what we'll do. We'll look at each other and see the great things we saw in the people we cared about. And we'll make believe as it comes along.'

Aiden felt a wave of something resembling fear cross his chest. 'Yes.'

CHAPTER SIX

WITH Mick and Joe assigned to Aiden the next day Caitlin found herself in the company of John and Louise—aka Lou.

Caitlin was more silent in their company. But not because they weren't nice people. It had more to do with a distinct lack of a decent night's sleep.

After their 'truce' Caitlin and Aiden had spent the rest of the afternoon and the evening looking at photos and videos of her family while she explained who they all were. She'd talked about growing up with her sister and two brothers, about childhood holidays and what they were all doing with their lives now, as grown-ups. And all the while she'd been aware of the fact that he didn't have memories like hers.

But she hadn't asked questions about his childhood until they had once again been lying in the darkness on opposite sides of the hall. Somehow it was easier like that. With the silence that only nighttime hours brought. Without having to look each other in the eye. Like being covered in a dark comfort blanket.

And she'd needed that blanket as he'd talked with that deep masculine voice of his, the tones hypnotic and soothing, and told her about growing up in his many different 'families'. About early Christmases when he'd hoped Santa would bring him his own parents, and about teenage resentment that others had it easier than he had.

He claimed to have come past it all, to have grown determined to make his life better, no matter what his start had been. But the old scars ran deep. Even when he'd tried to make jokes about things that broke her heart at the childhood he'd lost. For hours she'd wanted to reach out to the small boy, to hold him close and show him the kind of love she'd had when she was little.

But that boy was gone.

She'd thought about it long after the conversation had faded away and she'd heard Aiden's breathing even out and deepen as he fell asleep.

And she'd thought more about how he'd managed to become the person he was now. *Who* the man was. She was learning about the simple things, like how he took his coffee and his liking for 'simple' cuisine. But it didn't delve much below the surface. He was still Aiden Flynn man of mystery. And that was still intriguing her.

The thing was, she couldn't allow herself to become too fascinated by him, could she? This wasn't a new relationship that could grow naturally and possibly even end in friendship, or something. Because once the show ended he'd be gone. And the very fact that their paths had never crossed before just proved how different their worlds were in reality.

Driving to her family's home in the bright autumn sunshine, she frowned from behind her sunglasses. Despite the fact that they were finding at least a small way of communicating, the fact remained that there was still something there that had them both on edge with each other. And this new agreement, to treat each other as they would have partners they'd cared about before, only put her more on edge.

She pulled the car into the gravel driveway of the family home in the countryside, an hour from Dublin. She switched off the engine and sat for a moment looking at the front door. Every scrap of security she carried through her adulthood had been cultured inside those walls. Here she had grown up with a support network that had made her stronger by the simple fact that she knew she wasn't alone in the world. No matter what mistakes she made or what bad things happened. There was always home. And sets of arms ready to enfold her.

Selling this house wouldn't just be selling bricks and mortar. It would be giving away a million memories and leaving behind some of the warmth and love of her family in the walls. She just couldn't let it happen.

With a small glance at the camera she removed her sunglasses and smiled bravely. 'This is where the real test begins.'

The three of them walked up to the large red door. But before she could sound the bell the door swung open and she was tugged inside by her eldest brother. 'About bloody time! What did you do, Cait? Walk from Dublin?'

She hugged him back as he pulled her into his arms. 'Ha-ha. Not all of us drive like we're in the Monte Carlo Rally.'

Connor's driving was a source of much debate in the family. He felt he was very safe. Everyone else felt there wasn't that big a rush to get to places.

Setting her back at arm's length again, he examined her face and then grinned. 'You look tired. Aiden keeping you up at night?'

Caitlin blushed a fiery red and thumped him in the chest. 'None of your business.' She glanced down the large hall to where sounds of voices filtered through. 'Everyone here? Aiden shouldn't be long. He's driving himself up. Stuff to do in town today.'

'Oh, he's already here. It's just Cara we're waiting on.'

Aiden was already here? On his own? On his own in the lions' den? *Dear Lord.* Her family would only need to grill him for about half an hour and he'd fold under the pressure! What was he thinking?

'How long has he been here?'

''Bout an hour, I think. He said you told him half-seven.'

'I said half-eight.' She'd said it at least four times at breakfast. He'd done this on purpose.

Sidestepping Connor, she walked swiftly down the hall into the huge family room where everyone usually gathered before dinner. There were greetings all round, hugs and the odd jibe about her 'secret lover', but no Aiden.

She did a quick head-count. 'Uh, where's Mum?'

Connor's wife winked across at her. 'In the kitchen grilling Aiden, of course.'

Caitlin turned round so quickly she almost knocked over her eldest nephew behind her. In a flash she caught him, and picked him up for a swift hug. 'Hey, Danny. Still my favourite nephew?'

The child grinned at her as she set him down. '*Only* nephew, Auntie Cait.'

She patted him on the head, her eyes already looking out through the doorway. 'Still my favourite, though.'

'Is Aiden gonna be my uncle?'

She blinked down at him and felt a wave of guilt. 'Not if your nanny steals him first, honey.'

'I like Aiden. I think I'll call him Uncle Aiden.'

Her heart twisted and her voice wobbled a little as she ruffled his hair. 'I'm sure he'd like that.'

'I'm gonna go ask him!' He scooted away from her hand and ran into the hall.

Caitlin followed with swift steps. The situation was getting out of control.

'Whoa, there!' Aiden laughed as the child ran straight into his legs. Bending down for a second, he set him back a step. 'Ask me what, kiddo?'

Caitlin stopped dead in her tracks and stared, her voice faltering. 'He wants to know if he can call you ''Uncle Aiden''.'

Aiden stood upright and looked at her face, something flickering across his eyes.

Caitlin just stood statue-still and stared. Her heart sped up fast in her chest and her breathing changed.

Holy Moly. What in God's name had he *done* to himself?

She swallowed hard. The beard had gone. She blinked slowly. He'd changed his clothes too.

Her eyes continued to study him in minute detail. He'd had a haircut. The Aiden Flynn who had landed on her doorstep not forty-eight hours ago wouldn't even have turned her head in the street. But this guy? This guy was a completely different kettle of fish.

The dark blue stripes in his lighter blue shirt made his eyes even bluer. If that was at all possible. And his unruly hair was now cut so that the shorter curls hugged his head, giving him the look of a mischievous child. That mischievous edge was only backed up by the fact that he had deep dimples that made grooves in his cheeks as he grinned at her. Dimples, for crying out loud!

She swallowed again. Aiden Flynn man of mystery was out and out, hold the horses, call the cavalry *gorgeous*. Who'd have thought it?

He continued grinning at her over the couple of feet that separated them. 'Hey, you're late.'

Finally finding something else to focus on, she lifted her chin an inch and answered with, 'No, memory man, you're early. We said half-eight.'

'Did we?' He blinked innocently at her.

'Yes, we did.'

'Whoops.' Ruffling Danny's hair, he stepped towards her. 'I guess I just couldn't wait to meet everyone.'

Her eyes remained focussed on his face as he got closer, then closer. She stepped back a step. *The prey trying to escape from the predator.*

Okay. Possibly a tad dramatic. But it was how she felt.

Something thumped into her back and, turning her head, she found an apologetic John looking at her. 'Sorry.'

She'd actually forgotten for the briefest moment that the crew were even there. Turning back towards Aiden, she tilted her head to look over his shoulder as Mick looked out from behind the lens to wink at her.

Danny pointed up at Mick. 'These are Aiden's cameras.'

Aiden's head snapped towards him. 'They're not mine, Danny.'

'You bringed them.'

'No, they just came *with* me.' He frowned and then improvised and pointed towards Caitlin. 'See—Auntie Caitlin bringed some too.'

Danny waved at John. John waved back.

'Is that Caitlin out there?' Her mother's voice sounded from the kitchen behind Aiden.

'Yeah, Mum, I'm here.'

'About time too. Come on in here and help me with this roast, would you?'

Caitlin blinked. She had spent years training to cook, and even though she was damned good at what she did her mother still ruled the home kitchen like Attila the Hun.

She never asked Caitlin to help. Ever.

Aiden saw the look on her face and took a step closer, his voice lowering. 'It's okay. Go on. It's been fine so far. I haven't done anything wrong.'

Looking up at him, she smiled weakly. 'You wouldn't know yet if you had.' Then she whispered, 'Trust me.'

With a deep breath and a straightening of her dress for added confidence she stepped past him. And then past Mick and Joe.

Aiden nodded at John and Lou, who set down tools and left with a wave. Then with a similar deep breath Aiden walked into the family room.

'It's not like you to ask for help, Mum.'

'Well, if it's the only way I can get you to talk to me then I have to ask for help, don't I?'

Moving up beside her, Caitlin looked down at the perfect roast. 'I only just got here.'

Her mother placed a warm kiss on her cheek and an arm over her shoulders for a hug. 'I've been talking to your Aiden.'

Caitlin smiled weakly.

'He seems a very nice young man.'

She turned her head and blinked.

'Even though it is a bit of a surprise to us all.'

And here it came. Test number one.

CHAPTER SEVEN

'BUT if you're happy then we're happy.'

The words couldn't have surprised her any more if she'd said she'd been thinking of taking up pole dancing. What on earth had he done to win her mother round so fast?

The arm squeezed her shoulders again. 'You are happy, aren't you, pet?'

Smiling a wide smile that she genuinely hoped looked convincing, Caitlin raised an arm to her mother's waist and squeezed back. 'I am, Mum. Really.'

Eyes so similar to her own searched for a long second and then she smiled. 'Good.' Then she laughed. 'He is simply gorgeous, isn't he?'

Mmm. *Who knew?*

'Yes.' She blushed. 'He is.'

Removing the arm, she went back to her roast and shooed at Caitlin with an oven glove.

'Now, away off and keep him company in there.'

Glancing across one more time, Caitlin turned and left the room. Her mum was usually the suspicious member of the family. The 'carefully does it' one. But Aiden had won her over inside an hour. It truly was amazing the difference a shave and a haircut could make.

In the family room he was laughing with Connor as Patrick, the second youngest of her siblings, told one of his many tales.

Aiden looked up and reached an arm out for her. 'Hey.'

With a moment of hesitation she took his hand. Then stepped closer, planning on sitting on the arm of his chair.

But Aiden apparently had different ideas and tugged her hand until she was in front of him. Then pulled her down onto his lap.

She landed with a small thump and turned her head to look at his profile. 'Sorry.'

'It's okay.' He smiled, 'I wasn't planning on ever using my legs again.'

'Yeah, heavy lump, isn't she?'

She glared at Connor. 'Funny.'

'Actually, considering her occupation, it's amazing she doesn't weigh about twenty stone,' Aiden continued, smiling.

Patrick laughed. 'Have you ever actually *eaten* anything she's cooked?'

'Spoken by the guy who eats at least twice a week anywhere I work.'

'What can I say?' Patrick shrugged. 'The family discount is good.'

Caitlin let out a small snort of laughter. 'And the fact that you burn a boiled egg doesn't encourage you to eat at home much.'

He came back with an equally derogatory remark, which completely went over Caitlin's head. Instead she was distracted by the way Aiden had twined his long fingers with hers, his thumb rubbing across the flesh at the base of her thumb.

She turned her head and looked into his eyes.

His smile was slow, intimate. Burning in its intensity. And his dimples reappeared.

Caitlin squirmed slightly on his lap and his smile grew.

Leaning his head close to her ear, he whispered, 'I wouldn't do that too much, if I were you.'

Her cheeks flamed.

'Hey, you two.' Patrick interrupted them. 'There are kids in this room!'

'Oh, leave them be, Pat,' Connor's wife Jane rocked the newest member of the family in her arms and looked over from the sofa. 'They can't help it if they're in love.'

'And how exactly do you think those kids got into the world in the first place?' Connor winked.

'I don't need to know, thank you.'

'Some day you'll have to look into how it's done, though.' Connor leaned forward as he smiled. 'You can't leave all the grandkids to me and Jane. Or these two.'

A thumb jerked in Aiden and Caitlin's direction.

'Yes, you'll need to get going on that fairly soon. Take some of the pressure off us.' Jane smiled.

Brendan, quiet in his usual large armchair in the corner, leaned forward and interrupted the banter. 'You both want a family?'

'Dad!' Caitlin avoided his piercing stare by glancing at Aiden. 'We're not even married yet.'

'But you'll have discussed it.' He paused. 'In all those internet talks.'

'Chats, Dad.' Patrick smiled. 'They're called chats.'

Brendan ignored him. 'But you'll have talked about it.'

Caitlin faltered.

Aiden squeezed her hand. 'Yes, we've talked about it.'

'And?'

He turned and looked the older man in the face. 'Yes, we want kids. Family is important to both of us.'

'You come from a big family, Aiden?'

Her heart caught at the question. 'Dad—'

Aiden looked up at her. 'No, it's okay. It's no big deal.'

She continued watching him as he turned his face back towards her father.

'I don't have any family. My mother and father never married and I hadn't met my father until a year ago.'

Brendan continued to stare at him. 'You see them?'

'No, sir. My mother died when I was five, and my father about six months ago.'

Caitlin opened her mouth to say something. Then she looked around the room at her family, and at Mick and Joe, and the words died away. She couldn't talk about this new information in front of them all. Because she was 'engaged' to Aiden. She already knew all this—right?

Instead she squeezed his fingers.

He didn't look at her. His free arm simply lifted and he placed a hand against her back, smoothing his fingers in small circles. *It's okay* he was telling her. And she understood.

'You were adopted, then?'

'No.' He smiled. 'Problem child.'

'In what way?'

A shrug. 'I guess you could say I had anger management problems.'

'Still got a temper?'

'I outgrew it.'

Brendan's eyes narrowed imperceptibly. 'Glad to hear it.' He leaned back in his chair. 'Don't think I'd be too happy if my child married someone with an uncontrollable temper.'

'Neither would I if someone like that married my daughter.'

There was a nod. 'You'll understand what it's like when you have a daughter of your own.'

'I hope we'll have lots of them.' Aiden paused and then looked up into Caitlin's eyes. 'Girls with big brown eyes.'

Caitlin blinked at him with her big brown eyes. He was good. Many a one would have baulked under her father's inquisition. But not Aiden. He'd come right out and been forthright with him about his family. And with one glance had probably persuaded the entire room that he wanted nothing more than a team of miniature Caitlins. That somewhere inside he'd already mentally pictured them.

Trouble was, for the briefest second she could see them too. But in her head they had the bluest of eyes. And dimples.

'Dinner's ready. Where's Cara?' Maggie Rourke smiled from the doorway.

'It's going well, isn't it?'

Freeing her hand from his, Caitlin walked across the patio and looked out on the dimly lit garden. It was the first chance they'd had to talk alone since the start of the evening. Even Mick and Joe had stayed inside, continuing to film her family's reaction to its latest addition.

'So far.' She turned to face him and sat down on the low stone wall that separated the patio from the lawn. 'But Dad and Cara had their heads together for a long time after dinner.'

'Your sister doesn't like me much.'

'Right now I don't think she likes me much better.'

'How come?' He walked over and sat down beside her, his body close to hers.

Caitlin had to fight the urge not to move away. Her family could still see them through the large glass doors, and it wouldn't look right if she jumped away from him the second he was close.

But she was still adjusting to the new Aiden. The Aiden who looked like every red-blooded single female's idea of *hot stuff*. The Aiden who had her pulse beating nineteen to the dozen every time he held her hand or smiled at her with those bloody dimples of his.

She was not going to be swayed by how he looked now. For one it would make her superficial, and she hated that. Because the long-haired, bearded Aiden hadn't even turned her head. Alternately irritated, flustered and surprised her, yes. But he hadn't affected her *physically*.

Not that he'd ever actually touched her before.

But before she'd been only too aware that the chances of them remaining friends after the show were at best remote. Now she had to be realistic and know that also meant being attracted to him was a dead-end street too.

And anyway, this just wasn't him. He wasn't this easy on the eye in real life. The show had done this. She just needed to remember that.

'Caitlin?'

She swallowed to damp her dry throat and tried to ignore where his hard thigh touched hers. 'Sorry—what?'

He nudged her shoulder with his. 'You all right?'

'Yes.' She smiled a little shyly at him. 'I'm fine. Just tired, I guess.'

'It's hard having to think so much around them.'

'Yes, it is.'

'So what's up with Cara, do you think?'

Caitlin sighed. 'I've hurt her.'

'Because of me?'

A nod answered him.

'How?'

She frowned, looking down at the paving as she thought how to word her answer. It was dark on the patio. Almost like it was when they talked across the hallway. So it was somewhat easier to talk it out. 'We always talk. About everything. No secrets. Ever. We talk every single day about everything, from the weather to the state of world peace and every little thing that's happening in our lives.'

Aiden understood straight away. 'But I was a secret, as far as she's concerned?'

'One I would never have kept from her.'

Aiden studied her bent head. 'I've come between you.'

'Yes, you have.' She smiled sadly at him as she turned her face towards his. 'And allowing that to happen is going to be all the more difficult to explain when I have to tell her this is all a lie.'

He reached out a long finger and brushed her errant fringe out of her eyes, studying her hair as he did so. Then his eyes looked into hers. His voice was soft. 'I understand how tough this is for you now that I've seen you with them.'

She tried hard not to let her heart beat out of rhythm as he spoke.

'What you all have here is precious.'

Her eyes welled. He of all people would see that.

'And I may not understand how badly you want a restaurant to go through all this. But I do know if it's something that important to you they'll understand. And they'll forgive you.'

A traitorous tear rolled out of one eye and streaked along her flushed cheek. She wanted to tell him the truth. She would never have done this to her family if it had been for as unimportant a thing as a restaurant of her own. She could never have been that selfish.

But even as she opened her mouth to tell him he was reaching out and wiping away the tear. The heat from his fingers burnt through her skin and straight into her bloodstream.

She could *not* fall for him.

His voice was low, sensually intimate. 'Don't cry, Caitlin Rourke. It'll be okay. I promise.'

Reaching a hand up, she removed his fingers from her cheek and smiled down at them. 'Don't make promises you can't keep, Aiden.'

'You need to trust me on this one.'

She tried to let go of his fingers but he turned his hand and tangled them with hers. 'They're still watching us, you know.'

Caitlin nodded. 'I know.'

'And I don't have a beard now.'

Her lashes flickered upwards as her eyes met his again. 'I got that. What are you—?'

He smiled at her as her eyes widened with realisation. Then he moved his face towards hers. 'I told you this would have to happen at some point.'

And before she could think of a reason for it not to his mouth descended onto hers.

CHAPTER EIGHT

SHE froze. The warmth of his lips against hers created ripples of heat across her body.

For a long time they just stayed that way. Their mouths locked together, their breath intermingled in the cool night air. It was as if time slowed down and the world became still. The sounds from the house were a million miles away.

Caitlin opened her mouth a little and let out a tiny sigh. The world of make-believe was a wondrous place. The pretend romance a beautiful place to be lost in. She'd make herself remember it wasn't real in a moment. In just another little moment.

Aiden felt the sigh against his mouth. It shook him to the soles of his feet. He told himself he'd been prepared for this. That kissing Caitlin for the sake of realism was something he could handle like an adult. An uninvolved, uncomplicated by emotions adult.

But she was getting to him. From the vulnerability that had tugged at his heart seconds ago to the sudden wrench in his gut as he felt the pull of attraction to her.

Kissing her had always been on the agenda. It was just a tick on the list of things to make the lie more convincing. That was all it was supposed to be.

It wasn't all it was.

The sigh was almost like a signal. One he interpreted as *Don't stop, Aiden.* So he moved his mouth across hers. Felt her move with him. His free hand moved up to her cheek while his other hand tangled with hers, their joined hands lifting in the air to dance together.

But deepening the kiss with a small tug of his teeth against her bottom lip made his body come to life. And that shook him.

Dragging his mouth from hers, he watched as her heavy eyelids finally opened. She looked at him with wide, mesmerised eyes. And he couldn't stop looking back.

The glass doors opposite them slid open and Caitlin's mother appeared. 'It's late. There's no point in you driving back to Dublin now. So I've made up Caitlin's room for you both.'

Caitlin's head snapped round to look at her. 'We can't share a room!'

Her mother looked surprised. 'Why on earth not?'

Glancing at Aiden, she found him staring at her with those hypnotic eyes of his. He didn't open his mouth to help out.

'You didn't like it when I shared a room with Liam any time he stayed, Mum.'

'You were younger then.' She smiled at Aiden. 'It takes a while for any parent to accept the fact that their children are all grown up in that department.'

Aiden managed to smile back while his mind searched frantically for a reason not to share a room with Caitlin. Not just a room but a bed too, he assumed. It was tough to find an excuse, though, while his damned libido kept picturing her curled in against him. He swallowed hard,

'We really don't mind separate rooms, Mrs Rourke. It is your house after all.'

'Please, Aiden. It's Maggie.' Her smile widened at his respect for her feelings. 'And it's nothing to worry about. Anyway, Cara is staying too, so she'll have the boys' room.'

Caitlin felt ill. She absolutely couldn't share a room with Aiden. Not after that kiss. She wouldn't be able to sleep a wink!

'We should get back to Dublin, Mum. It won't take that long.'

But her mother had the determined streak that Caitlin herself had inherited. 'Nonsense, dear. You're staying. I won't hear another word about it.'

They both stared up at her.

'Anyway, Aiden was saying earlier he wanted to take a look around here for somewhere to have the wedding. So we can have a look around tomorrow, after breakfast.' She stepped back towards the doors. 'Now, come on back in, you two, before you catch a chill.'

'We'll be right there.' Caitlin needed a moment to gather herself together. And to find a reason *not* to stay.

'Well, I'll leave the door open, so don't be long.'

'We can't share a room.'

Aiden knew it wouldn't be too great an idea. But Caitlin's determination that it shouldn't happen brought a frown to his face. 'We're not getting out of it too easy.'

She continued looking through the door, her voice low. 'I'll tell her I have to work tomorrow.'

'You already told them earlier you have a couple of days off.'

'Then I'll say I'm not feeling well.'

'Isn't she *more* likely to make you stay then?'

Caitlin turned and glared at him. 'Then *you* think of a reason!'

'It's only for one night, for crying out loud.' His frown promoted itself to a scowl. 'I'm fairly sure I can manage not to jump all over you.'

'It's not a question of you jumping all over me.'

'Then what is it?'

How could he possibly understand? There was far more intimacy involved in just being close to him. Especially considering what had just happened. And how it had made her feel. But then if he hadn't felt it too it really wasn't that big a deal to him, was it?

She skirted past the question and answered with a resigned, 'You'll have to sleep on the floor, then.'

'You told me you used to share the room with Cara. That means two beds, doesn't it?' He was asking for himself as much to calm her.

'It did. Until we both moved out and Mum had the room redecorated so couples could come to stay.'

'As a guest, doesn't that mean I should get the bed?'

'Fine. Sleep where you want, then.' She stood up and walked through the doors, pulling them shut behind her.

Her father looked at her with questioning eyes and she pinned a smile to her face. Then, with a quick glance around the room, she found a space between Patrick and Jane where she wouldn't have to sit by Aiden.

She didn't even glance his way when he opened the doors and came in after her.

'Well, we'd better get these wee ones off to bed, then.'

Jane stood up and handed her daughter into Connor's waiting arms.

Caitlin jumped up. 'Must you? It's been ages since I saw you.'

If they left then it would be one step closer to bedtime. She'd do anything to put that off.

'These two are up well past their bedtime.' Jane leaned over and kissed her cheek. 'We'll have plenty of time together with all the wedding stuff to come.'

'There's still no hurry on all that.' Brendan stood up. 'Plenty of time for a ceremony.'

'Actually, we've already set a date.'

Several pairs of eyes swept in Aiden's direction.

'You have?' Brendan's eyes narrowed. 'When, exactly?'

'The Saturday before Christmas.'

'That's less than three months away.' Maggie Rourke looked stunned. 'We can't put a wedding together that fast!'

Patrick laughed. 'You make it sound like such a big deal. It's only a wedding, for goodness' sake. A dress and a bit of a cake. What else do you need?'

Maggie frowned at him. 'Actually, there's a great deal more to it than that. There's guest lists, flowers, cars—a venue for the reception. And most of those places are booked up a year in advance, you know.'

'We don't want a big wedding, Mum.'

'Why on earth not? All of the family will want to be there, and you have so many friends.'

Caitlin shook her head. 'No, just something small will do us. No big fuss.' The thought of a fuss made her want to vomit.

Maggie looked as if she might cry. 'But it's the biggest day of your life! We always planned on giving our girls the best send-off. It's our job.'

And one they could ill afford. Glancing at her father's face, she wondered how much her mother actually knew. But Brendan's face was an impassive mask.

'No. We'll be footing the bill ourselves.' She stared across at Aiden. 'Won't we, darling?'

Darling? His eyebrows rose slightly. 'Yes, we're paying for it all. There's no problem there.'

Brendan looked him straight in the eye. 'No. We'll take care of it.'

'Dad, you can't—'

'Yes, I can—and I will. No daughter of mine is paying for her own wedding.'

'But, Dad—'

'I'll not hear another word.' He held up his hand. 'That's an end to it. But it'll not be in three months' time. We'll aim for June next year.'

Aiden opened his mouth to speak, but Caitlin got there first. 'Yes, it will, Dad.'

Brendan's eyes sparked at her. 'And what exactly is the rush? Are you pregnant?'

She blushed. 'No, I'm not pregnant.'

He nodded curtly. 'Then June it is.'

Her chest cramped as she continued to argue with him. 'No. We've made up our minds.'

He stared at her with angry eyes.

Aiden stepped between them, his back to Caitlin as he kept his voice low and determined. 'We want to get married as soon as possible.'

'Why?'

'We don't see any point in waiting. We know we want to be together, and waiting 'til June isn't going to change that. We both know life's too short.' He raised his chin an inch and squared his shoulders. 'And if there's a question of paying then I have it covered. I want to give Caitlin whatever she wants.'

He couldn't have said anything worse if he'd tried. Caitlin closed her eyes in anguish. Not only had he just dented her father's pride on the money issue, he'd also in a roundabout way suggested that Caitlin's wishes were more important to him than they were to her parents.

'You have a lot to learn about how this family works, young man.' Brendan held his anger in check, instead turning and walking out of the room.

The remaining inhabitants of the room stayed in a stunned silence. Caitlin opened her eyes and looked round at them all.

When she eventually spoke her voice trembled. 'We don't mean to upset anyone. We just want to get the ceremony over with, that's all.'

Aiden turned to look at her. 'So we can get on with the rest of our lives.'

His words were true on many levels. And even though she wanted to take the tension out of the room by just opening her mouth and admitting the truth the very fact that her father was so torn on the subject of paying for her wedding made her all the more determined to see it through.

'Yes.' She walked over to stand by him, her hand reaching for his to show a united front. He didn't know the damage he'd just caused. It wasn't his fault. She'd chosen to weave herself this web. 'We just need to get married.'

Maggie walked forward and placed one hand on her shoulder. 'Don't worry, love. Your dad just has a lot on his mind at the minute.' She smiled at Aiden. 'Bit of pressure at work.'

With those words Caitlin immediately knew that her mother knew.

She turned her smile on Caitlin. 'We'll talk about it tomorrow, when he calms down.'

Breaking her contact from Aiden's warm hand, Caitlin wrapped her arms around her mother's neck and held her close. 'Everything will be all right Mum.'

'Of course it will, dear.'

CHAPTER NINE

HE GRUNTED a little as he turned over on the floor.

'Are you all right?' Caitlin asked from above his head.

'Oh, yeah. Just dandy.'

She felt ridiculously guilty as she snuggled under the duvet. With only a throw cover to protect him from the wooden floor, he couldn't possibly be 'dandy'.

'Do you think you'll sleep?'

No. Not unless someone hit him over the head with something. But there was no way he was letting her sleep on the floor either.

'I'll be fine.'

Caitlin knew he wouldn't. It was ridiculous. Did she honestly think she would sleep any better knowing how uncomfortable he was than she would if he was beside her?

'You could try sleeping on top of the duvet, I guess—'

'Yes, I could!' He was off the floor and on the bed before she'd even finished speaking.

Caitlin frowned as he jostled the bed, getting into a comfortable position. In a couple of minutes he sighed with contentment. 'See— now, where was the problem?'

Lying as still as she could manage to, she gritted her teeth. 'Well, just don't try stealing any covers.'

'Wouldn't dream of it.'

They lay in silence for what felt like hours.

'You asleep yet?'

'Yes.'

He smiled in the darkness. 'Want to talk for a while?'

'I want to sleep.'

'You can't, though, can you?'

She sighed. 'No.'

'I upset your father tonight, didn't I?'

'We both did.' She rolled onto her side, facing him. 'He's a very proud man.'

'I'll bet if he pays out any money for the wedding the producer of the show would get it back to him.'

'Probably. I don't see why they wouldn't.' Explaining that to her father now wasn't an option, though.

'We could check it out, and that would solve that.'

She thought again about telling Aiden the facts. But her father's pride had taken enough of a denting tonight. If the show and the country found out why she was really doing this he would never forgive her. No matter how noble her intentions.

'They're not exactly rolling in money, Aiden. A wedding like the one they're talking about doesn't come cheap. And I don't think I could live with myself if they borrowed money for it.'

'Then we have to persuade him that *we're* paying for it. One way or another.' He mulled over the problem for a few silent minutes. 'How about if we just went ahead and booked it all without them?'

'Then my mum will kill me for leaving her out.'

'But I guess that's the whole thing about it, isn't it? The show is about how we get round all this.'

'Yes, it is.'

He shifted his weight and rolled towards her, just able to make out her shape in the darkness. 'How are you doing?'

The concern in his voice raised a small smile. 'I've been better.'

'Still worried about whether they'll forgive you for all this?'

'Yes. I knew lying wouldn't be easy. But I never knew it would be this tough.'

'Well, you know you can sound off to me any time you want. I'm not going anywhere.'

Her head nodded against the pillow as she tried hard to see his face in the darkness. 'I know.'

'I'd offer a friendly, comforting hug, but I might end up on the floor again.'

It was tempting. The hug, that was. Not putting him back on the floor.

In the darkness he was Aiden her temporary friend. They could talk easily and freely. And there was the added bonus that she couldn't actually see him the way he looked now.

But not seeing didn't stop her from knowing.

And knowing led to mentally picturing what she couldn't see. And mentally picturing him with those bluer than blue eyes and those mischievous dimples of his only triggered the memory of his mouth on hers.

And now she was lying in bed with him. Inches from the first person she'd felt a serious physical attraction to since Liam. With not a damn thing she could sensibly do about it.

'Much as I need a hug, it's probably best it doesn't happen.'

'What's wrong? Don't trust yourself?'

That was exactly what it was. 'Right now we're in a vulnerable situation. It wouldn't be too good an idea to get used to relying on you for hugs.'

Aiden felt his gut twist at her words. He knew she was right. But he wanted to be there for her to lean on. To sound off to. To let go at when it was emotionally too tough for her to handle. And it wasn't like him to offer to allow a woman to cry all over him.

But not holding her close in a large double bed was probably the more sensible way to go. Considering how it had felt to kiss her.

'Not that a hug wouldn't help occasionally.'

Her unexpected words caught him off guard and he stayed silent.

Caitlin wanted to take the words back the minute they came out. They'd just sort of spilled over. She hadn't wanted to make him feel she didn't appreciate him trying to be supportive. She was glad he was the way he was. That they could have these talks away from the cameras and her family's prying eyes.

But to have actually invited him to hug her. Here and now. Where they were and after *that* kiss. She must be off her rocker.

And he'd gone quiet. He hadn't meant the offer to be accepted. She'd just made a complete fool of herself.

But even while she tried to think up some wisecrack to break the silence his voice sounded low beside her. 'Turn over.'

'What?'

'Turn over so your back is to me.'

'Why?' She felt her heart flutter dangerously.

'I believe its called ''spooning'' in some countries. It's a kind of a hug.'

She knew what spooning was. It wasn't just a hug. It was way more intimate than a hug. 'Aiden, I'm not sure…'

'I know you're not.' He moved closer. 'So I'm being forceful and taking charge. Roll over.'

She did what she was bid. Which probably surprised him as much as it surprised her. Then with another move of the bed his body was alongside hers and his arm circled her waist.

She could feel the warmth of him everywhere—from where his breath teased her hair to where his knees fitted in against the backs of hers.

Yes, there was a duvet between them. But it didn't mean she wasn't aware in every tingling nerve-ending on her body. He might as well have been lying naked beside her.

And *that* mental picture almost made a moan escape her lips. This was a *bad* idea.

'Better?' His deep voice sounded right beside her ear.

Her voice came out a little tense, even to her own ears. 'Uh-huh.'

They lay in silence for another while, then Aiden asked, 'So, apart from upsetting your father, how do you think we did?'

'Well, you were certainly a hit with my mother.'

His low laughter vibrated from his chest through to her back. 'I may have flirted with her a little.'

Caitlin turned her head towards him. 'You didn't?'

'She even blushed at one stage.'

'Stop!'

'I thought it was sweet. Must be where you get the blushing thing from.' He smiled at the outline of her head. 'You did that a bit to-night.'

She was doing it again, actually. 'It's an extremely annoying habit.'

'It's a part of what makes up you. And that makes it nice.'

'Because *I'm* nice?'

'Yes, you are.' He meant what he said.

'Nice is a kind of non-committal word. I'm not sure I like being described as *nice*.' She turned her head on the pillow again. 'There are several other words I could use that I would like better.'

'Like for instance...?'

'Well, you've spent some time with me now, so why don't you tell me and I'll let you know if I think you're right?'

Aiden thought about it some, and started with the safer ones. 'You're tall.'

'I'm five-eight—that's hardly Gulliver material.'

'Still, it's fairly tall. I like tall women.'

'Just as well, seeing you're engaged to one.'

'Mmm.' He tightened his arm slightly. 'You have a sense of humour.'

'Just as well, considering I'm engaged to you.'

'You're not afraid to speak your mind.'

'Neither are you.'

'At least we both know where we are that way.'

They didn't, though, did they? There were still plenty of things they held back from each other. 'In some ways.' She dived in with a question. 'Why didn't you mention you'd met your father?'

He shrugged against her. 'Didn't come up.'

'Did he come looking for you?'

'No, I found him. I needed to know what he was like, to know why he'd never tried to find me.'

She'd have done exactly the same thing if she'd been in his shoes, she guessed. To know your parents was to understand where you came from, what made up part of the person you were. Life experience certainly made up the main part of the picture, but the people who created you had things to add too.

'And what was he like?'

'Sick, by the time I got to meet him—which was a bit sad. I'd have liked to know him when he was younger, stronger. But there was enough there for me to see some of myself in him.'

She turned round a little more towards him, her hand coming to rest on his where it lay against her stomach. 'Why did he never look for you?'

'When he split from my mother it wasn't exactly amicable. He figured if I wanted to I'd find him some day. He was right. But it's not the way I would have done it.'

'What would you have done?'

'I'd have searched to the ends of the earth for my child, been there every time he needed me.'

Her heart twisted again for the child who had wanted his parents so badly. And she knew his softly spoken words were edged with determination. He would have beaten down doors to get to his own child. 'You'll make a great dad some day, Aiden.'

He rubbed his thumb against her hand. 'I hope so.'

She turned her face towards him again, could feel from the way her breath came back on her skin that she was close to him. 'I know so. You were great with Danny. He never normally takes to people that quickly.'

Aiden felt her sweet breath against his face and lifted his chin towards the source. 'That would be the cameras he thought I bringed. Kids love that.'

'Then all you need to do is work with TV cameras all the time and you'll never go wrong.'

He was glad she couldn't see his face.

'But it was more than that. You were relaxed with him. Open. Kids can see that.' She snuggled down a little. 'You'll be a great dad.'

'I just need to find a great mum, then.'

She smiled. 'Not while you're engaged to me, you don't.'

'No.' He lifted his hand from her waist and raised it to outline the side of her face. 'Not while I'm engaged to you.'

She must have been feeling more tired than she'd thought. The tender touch of his fingers against her cheek was something she should have turned away from. She shouldn't have allowed it to feel so natural to be touched by him. But her defences were down. 'I almost forgot the cameras were there tonight.'

'I know what you mean.' It was actually a compliment to his crew that it had felt that way. For a couple of moments during the evening he had even forgotten himself. Especially when he'd kissed Caitlin. And he should have been more aware of the cameras than anyone else. 'But there aren't cameras now.'

'No.' She continued staring at the shadows of his face, so very close to hers. 'All this is very real sometimes.'

'Yes.' His thumb moved to the edge of her mouth. 'Very real.'

'But getting involved with each other probably wouldn't be a good idea, would it?'

'Probably not.'

She moved her body a little closer. 'Because when this is over we'll probably never see each other again.'

When it was over she would probably never *want* to see him again. There were just too many lies.

'That's more than likely.'

She didn't answer him. Just stayed still beside him as his fingers caressed her skin and his thumb teased the edge of her mouth.

And without another word he forgot the sensible way to go and moved in to kiss her again, his mouth moving over her lips and encouraging her to participate. To forget everything for a little while.

Her hand moved up to touch his jaw, then around to the nape of his neck to hold him closer. And for a while there was no TV show, no lies and pretence. There were just two people who wanted to be close. In the darkness. In a bed made for intimacy.

It was all the reality they needed.

CHAPTER TEN

CAITLIN made her way downstairs while the house was still silent, wandering barefoot through to the kitchen with a smile on her face.

'Well, don't you just look like love's young dream this morning…?'

The sound of Cara's voice from the patio made her jump. Peeking outside, she found her already dressed and sitting on the low wall, with a coffee in one hand and a cigarette in the other. Caitlin frowned. 'I thought you quit smoking?'

'You know us Rourkes. We're no quitters.' Cara smiled sarcastically.

With a sigh Caitlin wandered outside and looked down into her sister's face. 'Are you going to spend the next few months hating my guts?'

'I dunno, sis. Are you going to spend the next few months lying to me?'

The question hit low in her stomach. 'Lying about what, exactly?'

'About this internet guy.' Cara took a draw from her cigarette and blew smoke into the air. 'There's something going on there that you're not telling us.'

She kept her face calm. 'Like what?'

Cara shrugged. 'I don't know yet. But there's something not right and I just know it.'

Caitlin stared down at her.

'So how come we've never heard anything about him before now?'

She thought fast on her feet. 'Not everyone likes to admit they met the right guy through the internet.'

'Maybe at the beginning. But by the time it was getting serious enough to be discussing marriage you'd have thought it might be time to mention something.'

'Maybe. But maybe I was so wrapped up in falling for him that I couldn't think straight.' And that wasn't entirely a lie. Having just spent the night wrapped in Aiden's arms, it was tough to focus on what was real and what wasn't.

Cara shook her head. 'I'm not buying that.' She flicked her cigarette and looked straight ahead. 'Anyone who's that in love does that whole glowing nonsense. They grin like an idiot and can't wait for someone to tell. And there was a time when I'd have been the first person.'

'I know you're hurt by that.'

Cara continued to look ahead and smoke as Caitlin moved over and sat beside her. She didn't even react when her sister's arm encircled her shoulders.

'I'm sorry I didn't tell you about all this.' She searched for words that would reassure without giving everything away. 'But I'm also sorry that you haven't taken the time to get to know Aiden.' She smiled. 'He's something when you get to know him.'

'A haircut and a shave have certainly helped.' Cara managed a half-smile. 'I'll give you that much.'

Caitlin laughed. 'Yeah, don't I know it?'

'I just don't get it, Cait. I'm sorry, but I don't. He's come out of nowhere and now you're going to be married before Christmas? What's the rush?' The smile faded. 'You know Dad doesn't have the money to put on a big wedding right now either.'

Caitlin's eyes widened in surprise. 'You know that?'

Cara shrugged. 'I'm not stupid. There's been stuff going on around here recently, and Mum keeps hinting about Dad's work worries. So I'm assuming that something's up.'

So she wasn't the only one who had noticed then. It was the first time that there'd ever been a family crisis that they hadn't all been involved in solving. It made her sad that they'd come to this.

'We can afford to pay for the wedding, Cara. That part's not a problem.'

'Your internet guy has money, then?'

Actually, she was fairly sure he didn't. He needed the money from this show—or why else would he be doing it? But it was an answer that would make sense to everyone. 'Yes, he has money. And his name's Aiden. It would be nice if you could try to remember that.'

Cara ignored the request and continued, 'Well, he's certainly confident enough to suggest he has experience of getting what he wants when he wants it. He had Mum wrapped round his finger in seconds. And everyone else doesn't seem to have even blinked an eye at him being here.'

'Because maybe he's not as much of a surprise to everyone else as you seem to think he should be.'

'But he's not exactly like Liam either, is he?'

Liam and Cara had adored each other—spent nearly as much time in each other's company as Caitlin had with him. And suddenly some of Cara's resentment towards Aiden made perfect sense. 'There would always have been someone else eventually, Cara. Surely you have to know that? I'm only twenty-eight years old. Liam wouldn't have wanted me to be alone for ever.'

Cara's hand shook slightly as she raised her cigarette for a final draw. 'I know that.' She exhaled and stubbed it out with her foot on the ground, 'But I guess I thought that I'd be as close to whoever it was as I was to Liam.' She smiled sadly. 'I still miss him.'

Caitlin's voice was soft. 'So do I. And there'll never be anyone I feel that way about again. There couldn't be.'

They sat in companionable silence for a few long moments. Then Caitlin squeezed Cara's shoulder again. 'But that doesn't mean I don't want a chance at feeling something just as strong with someone else.'

Cara turned her head and smiled. 'I know.' She squeezed Caitlin's free hand where it sat on her lap. 'And you deserve that, sis. You really do. You're too gorgeous to stay alone.'

Caitlin grinned. 'Yeah, what can I say? I know.'

Cara laughed. 'Big head.' But she knew Caitlin wasn't like that. Then her eyes grew serious again. 'Just be sure about this Aiden guy before you do anything you might regret, okay?'

'Okay.' Caitlin looked down at their hands, avoiding her sister's eyes.

It was good advice. Good advice she could probably have done with having said out loud before she'd allowed Aiden to hold her close in bed. She was already involved with him above and beyond the call of duty required for the show. So much for them being such complete opposites.

'I'll make an effort to get to know him, okay?' Cara leaned her head down slightly, to get back into Caitlin's line of vision. 'Just so long as you make an effort not to shut me out any more.'

Caitlin only wished she could. 'I'll make an effort.'

Aiden moved back through the doorway with silent steps. He hadn't meant to eavesdrop. But as he'd stepped into the kitchen he had overheard Caitlin talking with Cara and hadn't wanted to interrupt.

The last thing he'd heard had been Caitlin saying that she would never feel the same way about anyone else as she had about Liam.

And that had rocked him. Had hurt. Hurt when he hadn't believed it could have.

He frowned as he stood in the hallway. Why? Why did it matter that she felt that way? Because for a brief time they'd both let go of the fact they were playing out a role and allowed themselves to make it real? All it was was a couple of brief encounters. Not the basis for anything else.

How could it be?

He was supposed to be here to mix things up. To make it more difficult for Caitlin to convince her family that he was really her fiancé. That was his job. That way the viewer at home watching the show would be more interested in how she got around everything.

But he hadn't done any of that. The conflicts already existed. Emotions for everyone were already running close to the surface. Even without his own sudden personal input to the whole mix. Which had never been intended in the original plan. Yes, he had always planned on being himself as much as possible. He was a producer, after all, not an actor.

The truth was that the intricacies of Caitlin's family and their obvious love for each other were just as fascinating to watch. And as easy to become involved in.

But he needed to detach himself personally from Caitlin Rourke. And the fierce emotions she brought to the surface. Because there was no point in it.

Because even if he was able to eventually reveal his role in all this and have her forgive him she was still in love with a dead man.

And that left him with no choice but to get back to work. To treat this like the professional project it was meant to be.

He squared his shoulders as he made his way back up to the bedroom to change. Enough of the make-believe.

CHAPTER ELEVEN

'WE DON'T want a big fancy do.' What did she have to do to persuade everyone of that?

'I think it would be nice.'

She frowned past her mother at Aiden. 'You do?' *He did?* 'Since when?'

Aiden shrugged. 'I think it would be nice for everyone we know to be there.'

Everyone they knew? How big a lie did he want this to be? She was having difficulty enough keeping up the pretence with just her family.

'I thought we agreed on something small and simple.'

'No, actually, we never made a decision on that.'

'Well, *I'd* prefer something small and simple.'

'Caitlin, a lot of people's feelings would be hurt that way.' Her mother was definitely on the 'big wedding' team. 'You have Uncle Bernie and Auntie Doris from the States. They're your godparents. You can't tell me you wouldn't want them there?'

Now they were going to fly people from halfway around the world for this farce? She could feel the walls of the Country Hotel closing in on her. Small and simple had always been the way she'd thought this would go. It would be the easiest option to get it over and done with. She should have known her large family would take a wedding seriously. It was what had always been planned with Liam.

'Mum...' She glanced in desperation at Aiden, her eyebrows rising when he glanced away. 'Mum—' she looked back at her mother '—this isn't giving people enough time in their schedules to come to this wedding. It's just before Christmas, after all, and they'll have made plans for Christmas, won't they?'

Aiden was silently proud of how she was trying to find a way out of this one. She was smart. She didn't really need him to help her out. Though really, if this wedding had been for real, he would have absolutely hated a big do. It wasn't as if he had a million people to bring along. Small and intimate would definitely have been his choice. Hell, just Caitlin and him on a beach somewhere would have done him.

He frowned as he realised he'd just thought about a real wedding with her. This needed to stop. 'There's still enough time for them to change their plans. The least you can do is give them the option. It's up to them whether or not they decide to attend.'

Caitlin's face was incredulous. What was he doing? She scowled as Mick circled her with the camera. 'Do you have any idea how many people we're talking about here? And let me tell you, Aiden, when they hear I'm getting married they'll come!'

'Then let them come.'

She wanted to kill him. It would be a circus. And the thought of standing in front of all those people and telling them it was a game...

Aiden watched as she went pale and felt a wave of guilt cross over him. But surely she'd thought about all these things before she took on the show? How could she not have known what her family would want? It wasn't as if they were the kind of people who would settle for a register office do. And the show wanted the whole hog, white dress and all, to make it convincing. It had been in the contract. The contract *she'd* signed.

'I think this place is perfect for a reception, Maggie.'

Maggie positively glowed at him. 'I'm glad you like it, Aiden. We've always liked the Country Hotel. Brendan used to play golf here a lot up until a few months ago.' She leaned closer to whisper. 'But the membership is quite steep.'

'This place doesn't come cheap.'

Aiden glanced at Caitlin and she glowered at him. 'That's not a problem. We have it covered, remember?'

If her father continued taking the standpoint that it was his duty to pay for the wedding then the cost of a reception alone in this place would sink him. Before they even added the cost of dresses and flowers…

'Well, you may sort that problem out with Dad before it gets any bigger.'

'Fine.'

'I mean it, Aiden.'

He looked her straight in the eye. 'Okay. I'll sort it out.' With a quick look at the concern on Maggie's face and the suspicion in Cara's eyes, he moved across and planted a kiss on Caitlin's cheek. 'You know you'll be happier with everyone here, honey. It's your special day. You don't need family arguments to ruin it.'

Caitlin blinked at him. He was playing the game. She knew that. But in doing what he'd just done he'd made it more complicated. He hadn't stood by her to keep it simple. She hated him for that. But she could play too. 'I only need you and me to make it special.' She looked at her mother and Cara. 'And those closest to me.' Then back at Aiden. 'But if you think this will work better then you need to talk to Dad. And soon.'

Before the nightmare got any worse.

'Right, then, that's sorted.' With his arm around Caitlin's waist he turned to look at Maggie. 'So, will we go and see if this place is booked for that date?'

In the space of one afternoon they had the Country Hotel booked for the reception, and for the ceremony itself. Her mother was like a child having a sugar attack. Talking nineteen to the dozen about invitations and guest lists.

'Cara, you'll book the time off to go with Caitlin to get dresses, won't you?' She asked the question as they got home. But it wasn't much of a question. More of an indirect order.

'I'm sure Cait doesn't need me to help pick her dress.'

'But it's your job as her bridesmaid—isn't it, Caitlin love?'

Cara walked straight through the kitchen and onto the patio, where she drew out a cigarette and lit it. 'I haven't been asked to be a bridesmaid.'

Maggie turned on Caitlin. 'Surely you'll be having Cara as your bridesmaid? Cara, and probably Isobel…'

Caitlin frowned at the mention of the best friend she had avoided calls from for the last few days. She was building up to telling her the glad tidings. Because Izzy was the person she spent most of her free time with when she wasn't with Cara. And it would be tough explaining a fiancé to her. Izzy was normally the one who was trying to push dates on her at every turn. She'd even succeeded a month back, when Caitlin had supposedly already met Aiden.

Under normal circumstances they were exactly the two people she would have asked to stand beside her.

'Of course I was going to ask Cara.'

'I'm not wearing anything frilly. Izzy won't wear frills either.'

Frills were the least of her damn worries. 'No frills. Gotcha.'

Keeping Izzy and Cara from getting together to discuss the timeline for her relationship with Aiden was going to be a nightmare.

'Then you girls could start looking at dresses next week.' Maggie walked over to fill the kettle. 'I'll speak to some printers tomorrow about invitations.'

'Great.'

'If you make up a list of the friends you want to invite, then I'll put together a list of the family.'

'Super.'

'I'd say you're probably looking at about a hundred guests, though, counting Aiden's friends.'

Caitlin's eyes widened. *'How many?'*

'Oh, at least a hundred. Our family alone will take you to about seventy.' Maggie turned from the kettle with a thoughtful look on her face. 'In fact, I suppose we could end up with a hundred and fifty.'

'A hundred and fifty?' She felt nauseous. 'You've got to be kidding, Mum!'

A hundred and fifty people for her to stand up in front of and confess to a lie as big as this one? She hadn't even been able to do bloody Public Speaking in school! She needed to find a way out of this, and fast.

'Have you met many of Aiden's friends?'

Caitlin blushed. 'Not really.' Her eyes wandered to the questioning look on Cara's face outside the door. 'We've been pretty wrapped up in each other.'

Maggie mulled over the information, then clapped her hands and grinned. 'We need to throw an engagement party!'

Oh, good God!

'We do not need an engagement party!'

'But it'll be the perfect way for all your friends to meet up. It's ideal.'

'No more expense, Mum. Enough is enough!'

'We could hold it here. It wouldn't cost that much.'

'Mum, I don't want an engagement party.' She frowned across at her mother. 'Seriously.'

'Anyone would think you were embarrassed about being engaged.' Cara blew smoke into the air as Caitlin looked out at her. 'You wouldn't like everyone to think you two had something to hide, would you?'

No. That was the last thing she would want anyone to think. Another wave of nausea crossed her stomach. She might actually genuinely be sick. Any minute now, in fact.

'There's nothing to hide.'

'Then we'll have a party here. Next weekend, I think. They'll give you time off work, I'm sure.' Maggie was already back in 'organising mode'. 'It'll need to be quick, with the wedding so soon. So as soon as you get back tonight start ringing round.'

'Okay.'

'I'll call Izzy, if you like.' Cara's voice sounded from outside again.

'No, its okay. I'll call her.' Caitlin pushed her chair back. 'I'd better get going, then. If I'm going to ring all these people tonight.'

And if she was going to avoid throwing up all over the kitchen floor. How on earth were they going to control that many people in one place at the same time? She needed to talk to Aiden, and fast!

'Ring me later with the numbers so I can organise the food and everything.' Her mother moved forward to kiss her cheek before leaning back and smiling warmly at her. 'Don't worry, love. We'll have all these things sorted out in no time. And then you and Aiden will be married.'

Caitlin managed a weak smile. 'Yes, Mum.'

'I'm so glad you found him, you know. It's what I've wanted for you for such a long time now.'

She felt her eyes well for the second time in as many days. 'I know.'

'And I'm sure Liam is smiling down on you right now, knowing how happy you are with Aiden.'

With another quick hug Caitlin pulled from her embrace and managed to make it to the hallway before the tears spilled over. She couldn't do this any more.

CHAPTER TWELVE

A<small>IDEN</small> frowned as he walked into his office at the network's main building in the city centre. Aisling was there, with half his team. 'So what's the emergency?'

Aisling had called him the moment he'd hit the city.

'We've got a problem.'

He faltered for a second. Just how much of him alone with Caitlin had they actually *got* on film?

'What kind of a problem?'

'Caitlin called me half an hour ago.'

'I only left her an hour ago.'

'Yes. She said.'

'So what's up?' He moved automatically into his seat behind the large desk.

'She wants out.'

The words knocked him completely off guard. 'What? Why?'

140

'She can't take the pressure of it all. The organising of the reception and this party her mother wants drove her over the edge.' Aisling stared at him. 'She was very upset.'

'What party?'

'Her mother came up with this idea for an engagement party next weekend. A chance for all your friends to meet each other.'

Aiden grimaced. That would be a tough room to play. Half his friends didn't even know he was doing the show. But they all knew what he did for a living. He'd have to forewarn them all so they didn't put their feet in it. It wouldn't be the first scheme he'd dragged them into…

He swore softly.

Aisling grimaced. 'Exactly.'

'We could hire some actors to play your friends, Aiden.' Tim, his junior assistant, piped up from the back of the room. He was enthusiastic about his job at the best of times and looked thrilled with his idea. 'It would be easier than using your own friends.'

'Yeah, but none of those actors would know me well enough in a week to be convincing.' He shook his head. 'I'll just have to be selective about who I invite.'

Aisling interrupted. 'It's not your friends that Caitlin's worried about.'

He nodded. 'If she's as close to her friends as she is to her family then emotionally that would be too much for her in one go.'

'You need to help her out.'

Aiden frowned as he looked around the room. He made a point of surrounding himself with a team he could trust. Creative people who weren't afraid to make their own input on any of the shows they put together. Flynn's Dream Team, as they were known. With eighty per cent of their shows polling in the top ten any time they came out, and dozens sold to UK networks.

They worked well together. And they'd always bounced ideas off each other. But he couldn't let them know he was getting emotionally involved on this one.

What he *could* do was tell them what he'd been thinking about on the trip home from Caitlin's with John and Lou. 'I think we need to rethink the way this show is going.'

'In what way?' Aisling pulled up a seat opposite him and the others sat where they could find space, ready for a debate.

'We went into this with the idea that I would set Caitlin up against her family for added interest.'

'To add to the conflict of it all.' Aisling nodded, 'You've been slow starting into that, though.'

He ignored her perceptive stare. 'I know. But in fairness I've only just met the family. I did add some today, with the reception and the wedding ideas.'

'And how did that go?'

'Well, it obviously worked if she's phoned and wants out.'

'But you don't feel too good about doing it?'

'We can't lose her now. There's too much invested in this.' Another voice sounded in the room.

'Exactly. So we need a rethink.'

'We could get her to actually fall for you. That would make it interesting viewing.'

Aiden chose to ignore the second voice. 'The thing is there's more than enough conflict going on with her family. I don't need to add to that.'

'So maybe you need to be more on Caitlin's side?'

'It's easier for her when I am.'

'So you think her family would be easier persuaded if you played the loving fiancé a little more?'

Aiden wasn't entirely convinced he could do that without getting more personally involved himself. By playing the loving partner and being her friend he could certainly help Caitlin more. But he'd be risking falling for her along the way. It was a big gamble for a TV show.

Aisling watched the emotions play across his face. 'You think that's the way to go?'

'I think she's probably going to walk out on this if I don't.'

'There's a penalty in the contract if she does.'

His stomach twisted as Tim grinned. He couldn't do that to her.

'She won't quit if I'm on her side.'

'You're that sure you can talk her round?' Aisling searched his face again. 'Even after just a few days? She was pretty upset on the phone.'

'I'm sure.' Though he felt like slime for knowing it would mean making his level of deceit even greater.

'Okay. Well, from what I've seen of the dailies you're right about the family conflict already existing. It makes for riveting viewing.' Aisling looked down at her notes. 'We just need to rework some of the commentary and we're still on a winner.'

Aiden nodded. 'Okay—we're in agreement, then.' He stood up, signalling the end of the meeting. 'I'd better go and see Caitlin.'

Aisling caught his arm as he was pressing the button for the lift. 'You okay?'

He smiled. 'I'm fine.'

She studied him again. 'Aiden, I've worked with you a long time. Don't try to lie. You're not that good at it.'

That brought a burst of sarcastic laughter. 'Oh, I think you'll find I am. I thought you said you'd watched the dailies?'

'I have. And that's why I'm asking if you're okay with all this.' She squeezed his arm as she continued, 'I've worked with you for five years now, and I've learnt more about you in three days of dailies than I ever knew before. You're opening up with her.'

His shoulders slumped slightly and he looked away from her prying eyes. 'I guess she just brings that out in me.'

'You like her?'

The dailies must have shown that too. 'Yes, I do.'

Aisling released his arm. 'You're coming out of a tough year, Aiden. I'm worried about you. I don't think you've dealt with all the stuff attached to your father. You're vulnerable right now. Maybe volunteering to do this show wasn't such a good idea.'

But then he wouldn't have got to spend time with Caitlin. It might mean much more of an emotional risk on his side than he could have foreseen, but he wasn't convinced he would have traded his time with her.

'Maybe talking things out with a stranger is exactly what I need right now.'

'She doesn't know about you, though. What you do or what you're supposed to be there to do. Do you think she'll understand when it comes out at the end?'

'I doubt it.'

She reached out and squeezed his arm again as the lift doors opened. 'Then be careful, boss man. It's only a TV show after all.'

He smiled and stepped into the lift. Only a TV show. Yes, that was all it was. Only his job. Only a career he'd fought hard for most of his life to have. All those things meant nothing compared to hurting Caitlin Rourke.

Just one small thing held him back from quitting it all and setting her free. After all, she was determined enough to eventually get the dream she wanted.

But this show wasn't just the one project. If he brought in this as a winner then he'd have a ticket to produce something that meant far more to him. He'd spent six months putting together the work that his father had spent a lifetime researching. It was the one tribute he could make to a man he had barely known. So the world would know who Donal Flynn had been, and could learn the amazing story of the history of one small part of the world he had loved.

It was the only legacy left by a man who had been so driven by his work that he had sacrificed love and family for it.

The question was, was Aiden driven enough to complete the work that he was prepared to sacrifice a piece of his own heart to do it?

'I can't do this.' Caitlin was determined. 'I've made up my mind, Aiden.'

'We can't get out of it. There's a clause in the contract that says we have to pay them if we quit after they start filming.'

She paled at his words. 'How much?'

'Nearly as much as they were going to pay us at the end of it all.'

Her eyes widened, her voice breaking. 'I can't pay that!'

'And neither can I. So we're stuck with this.'

What had she done? She'd gone into this to help her father out of his financial difficulty, and now she was trapped between failing and not making the money anyway, or quitting and having to pay out as much money as her father needed. And by quitting she'd put Aiden in the same position.

Moaning, she buried her face in her hands. 'What have I done?'

Looking down on her from the other side of the room, Aiden felt his heart twist at her anguish. If he weren't so tangled in the whole thing himself he would have told her the truth there and then and got her out of it.

He moved across and sat on the sofa next to her. 'We can do this if we work together.' He placed an arm across her shoulders and squeezed hard. 'Just think of your restaurant at the end of it. Isn't it worth it to get your dream?'

The shoulders beneath his arm shuddered and he heard a faint sob.

'Caitlin?' He reached his hand down and raised her chin with his fingers. The tears streaming down her face completely surprised him. 'What is it?'

'Oh, Aiden.' She smiled at him through her tears. 'I couldn't give a damn about getting a restaurant at the end. That's not why I'm doing this.'

Frowning in confusion, he looked up at the fixed camera on her living room wall before looking back into her pain filled eyes. 'I don't understand.'

'I know you don't.' She reached a hand up to link her fingers with his. 'And I'm sorry I didn't tell you earlier. I would have if it had just been about me. But it's not.'

'But if you don't want the money for a restaurant then what do you want it for?'

She shook her head and sobbed again. 'I can't tell you.'

He frowned harder, then took a second to think. 'Can't tell me or don't want to say on camera?'

Caitlin swallowed hard and whispered, 'The latter.'

'So it's not that you don't trust me?'

'No.' She squeezed his warm fingers again. 'It's not that. I think you know that by now.' Then she frowned a tiny frown. 'Though the lack of help with my mum today needs some explaining.'

'That doesn't matter right now.' He pulled her closer and tucked her head beneath his chin. 'Just tell me this. Will your family un-derstand why you did this at the end, when you tell them?'

'When they know what this show is really about then they'll know why I did it. But I'm not sure they'll forgive me any easier.'

He stayed silent as she turned her face into his neck and whispered in a shaky voice, 'I've made such a mess of this.'

The sobs returned, though they were a little muffled against his neck. And then Aiden did something that should have gone completely against his job as producer of the show. He set her back from him and stood, tugging her up off the sofa. 'Come with me.'

She blinked up at him as she was pulled to her feet. 'Where are we going?'

'Somewhere we can talk.' He left the room, pulling her behind him and up the stairs.

His eyes strayed to each of the remote cameras as he walked past them. He'd known where every one of them was from within a few hours in her house. Had even helped decide where most of them should go for maximum coverage.

But he had drawn the line at putting them in the bedrooms and bathroom. They needed some privacy somewhere. At the time it had been for the obvious things, like showers and getting dressed. He hadn't thought he would need camera-free zones for any other reason.

But now he was glad they were there.

Tugging her through her bedroom door, he closed it behind them and sat them both on the edge of her bed. He then held a finger against her mouth and whispered, 'There are no cameras in here, but they can still pick up normal speaking voices from the hallway.'

She frowned at him and removed his finger to whisper back, 'How do you know that?'

'I obviously asked more questions than you did.'

Thinking for a minute, she seemed to accept his answer.

'So why *are* you doing this if it's not to get your dream restaurant?'

The tears came again. 'I'm doing it for my father.'

Aiden frowned in confusion. 'You need the money for your father?'

She nodded, and he thought about the things that had been talked about in the last twenty-four hours. About how her parents couldn't afford a big wedding, how her father wanted to put it back to June. To have time to put the money together for it?

About her mother saying Brendan hadn't played golf at the Country Hotel in the last few months because it was so expensive. About Brendan's mind being on 'troubles at work'.

And it was suddenly very clear. 'His business is in trouble, isn't it?'

'Yes.' Caitlin gulped back a sob. 'How did you know?'

Aiden shrugged. 'I just figured it out. Stuff about the wedding expenses and his mind being on his work.'

A smile crossed her mouth. 'You really can be quite clever sometimes, can't you?'

With an answering smile he shrugged his shoulders. 'I have moments.'

'I don't want the world to know his business. It would kill him. He's a proud man.'

Another thought crossed his mind and he closed his eyes. 'Damn. All those things I said about paying for it all and having no problem with the money.'

She tangled her fingers with his, suddenly remembering he was still holding her hand. 'There's no way you could have known.'

His eyes opened. 'It hit him where it hurt most, though. That's why he was so angry with me.'

'With us.' She swallowed and looked down at their hands. 'Probably a little more at me, because he knows I know. And I was still pushing for an early wedding. That was worse than what you did.'

'Hell, honey.' He brought his other hand to her chin and once again forced her eyes up to meet his. 'I wish you'd told me sooner. I thought you were doing all this for some dumb restaurant.'

She blinked at him. 'Having my own restaurant isn't dumb. But it's not something I need to do this show to get. I would never have done something this hurtful to my family for personal gain.'

It was the one thing that he'd had the biggest problem with. Because it hadn't made any sense in the bigger picture that was Caitlin Rourke. The woman he was getting to know would never have done something that selfish. He'd known that almost instinctively. And it had bugged him that that was her reason.

Now he knew the truth. And it was as if she'd just given him the most amazing gift.

Because now he believed in her more than he'd ever believed in any single human being ever.

'You're amazing.'

Caitlin tilted her head at him, her eyes questioning. 'I am?'

'Yes, you are.' He freed his hand from hers so he could cup her face with two hands. 'You're the most selfless person I've ever met. You're prepared to go through all this heartbreak so that you can get your father out of trouble. To take a chance on making things right even though he might not forgive you for it. That's an amazing thing to do.'

Her bottom lip quivered as she looked into the bluer than blue eyes that were sparkling at her. 'But I can't do it, Aiden. I've failed.'

'No, you haven't.' He leaned forward and brushed his mouth across hers in a quick kiss. 'Because we're going to do this together. You and me. We'll make it work. And do you know why we'll make it work?'

She shook her head, mesmerised by his face so close to hers.

'Because it won't be hard to convince everyone that I'm crazy about you, Caitlin Rourke.' He leaned in close to her mouth again, his whispered words tickling against her sensitive lips. 'You see, I already am.'

CHAPTER THIRTEEN

THE party turned out to be not nearly half as bad as she'd thought it would be. But then a lot of the reason for that was Aiden, and how he stuck to her like glue for the evening. He would communicate with a touch of his hand, a squeeze of her fingers, or just by a smile or a twitch of his eyebrows. They hardly even needed words.

And that was pretty amazing in itself. They'd come such a long way in a few days.

Even the presence of the two camera crews in the room was soon forgotten beneath a little layering of food and alcohol. And Caitlin found herself relaxing for the first time since Aiden had knocked on her front door.

He leaned down to whisper in her ear before moving off to get them drinks from the buffet table. And that was when Izzy found her.

'I think you have a lot of explaining to do, young lady.'

Caitlin's heart caught at the softly spoken words. 'Yes, I guess I do. You probably hate me about now.'

'I should do.'

Caitlin smiled hopefully. 'And do you?'

Izzy studied her with a serious expression before cracking a smile. 'When you have that hunk of stuff on your arm and you look this happy?'

Caitlin breathed a sigh of relief and wrapped her arm around her friend's waist. 'Thanks.'

'And you do know you two are disgustingly happy, right?'

It was certainly the impression they were aiming for…

'He's pretty amazing when you get to know him.'

Izzy gave her a sidelong glance. 'And maybe now that I know about him I'll get the chance.'

Caitlin grimaced. 'I deserved that. I would have told you…'

'Mmm. Some time before I fixed you up on that date with Simon would have been good. You have to have already been talking to Aiden by then.'

In theory she would have been. 'It was early days then.'

'Any bit of a wonder you blew him off when you had *that* waiting in the wings?'

Avoiding her friend's perceptive eyes, Caitlin glanced across at Aiden on the other side of the room. It was funny how she was missing his presence by her side already.

A tall, fair-haired man appeared by him and they greeted each other with a manly hug. She smiled.

'So, what do I have to do to get you to forgive me on this, then?'

Izzy's face was glowing when she looked back at her. 'Well, you could start by introducing me to that gorgeous guy your fiancé is talking to.'

Caitlin nodded. 'Done.'

They started to move across the crowded living room. Then Izzy leaned her head down.

'And yes, by the way. I'd love to be your bridesmaid.'

'Who said I was going to ask?'

'Oh, you were. But, just so you know, I'm not wearing—'

'Frills. Yeah, I got that.'

Aiden glanced up as they approached and immediately smiled at Caitlin. Lifting one arm from his side, he invited her against his body. 'Hey.'

'Hey.' She smiled back at him. 'I brought my best friend to meet you. This is Izzy. Izzy, this is Aiden.'

Izzy shook the hand he offered her. 'The mystery fiancé. We meet at last.'

Aiden kept a smile on his face as he shook her hand. 'Indeed we do. I've heard a lot about you.'

Caitlin raised an eyebrow at him and he squeezed her waist gently, to let her know he knew. Izzy's name had never even been mentioned.

Izzy laughed. 'Oh I'll bet you have.'

'All good, of course.'

'Of course.' She released his hand and looked at the other man. 'And you would be…?'

'Mike.' The other man took his turn with the handshaking. 'I'm a friend of Aiden's from years back.'

'Then maybe you and I should get together some time, to compare notes on these two.'

Caitlin blanched at the idea. 'You can chat at the wedding.'

'Oh, I'm sure we'll all meet up before the wedding.'

Caitlin blinked at her. Oh, no, they wouldn't. It was difficult enough without everyone meeting to 'compare notes' when they weren't there…

'I have so many stories to tell about Caitlin that it would be a shame not to share them.'

'I'll lay odds that I have just as many about Aiden.'

Aiden frowned slightly at Mike. 'Stories you swore you'd never share with anyone.'

Mike leaned in closer to Caitlin. 'There's more to him than meets the eye.'

Caitlin smiled back at him. 'Do tell.'

'He will not tell.' The arm around her waist squeezed gently as he glared at Mike. 'Now, you wouldn't want Caitlin changing her mind before the wedding, would you, old friend?'

Mike smiled a small smile. 'Oh, no, we wouldn't want that. I'm sure she'll find out everything after the ''I do's''.'

Aiden could have merrily throttled him. But then of all his friends from the bad old days he'd guessed it would be Mike who would have the biggest problem with all this. It was just that the part of him that was now so attached to Caitlin had wanted Mike to meet her. Almost as if he was showing her off as his real fiancée and not some fake one.

Caitlin smiled up at Aiden and squeezed her arm tighter around his waist. This lying to friends thing couldn't be any easier for him than it was for her. But they had a united front now. The least she could do was support him in the same way that he was supporting her. 'I know as much as I need to know.'

Mike studied them both intently. 'It's good to see him with someone like you, Caitlin. You make quite a team.'

'Don't they just?' Izzy moved closer to his side. 'Doesn't it just give you the warm and fuzzies when people meet and fall in love?'

Mike smiled. 'Yes, doesn't it?'

'So...' She took a sip from her glass, batting her long lashes over its rim at him. 'You single, then, Mike?'

Caitlin grinned at her friend's subtlety. Izzy was moving in for the kill. Poor Mike didn't stand a chance.

Mike's eyes sparkled. 'In a sense, I suppose I am.'

Izzy seemed to glow beside him as she took another delicate sip of wine. 'And what is it you do, then?'

'Didn't he say?' Aiden grinned.

'No, I don't think so.'

Mike continued to look at her with sparkling eyes. 'I'm a priest.'

Izzy choked loudly on her drink.

*   *   *

Mike found Caitlin on her own on the patio nearly an hour later. He studied her from the glass doors for several long moments before speaking.

'You look like you have the weight of the world on your shoulders. Shouldn't you be grinning from ear to ear about now?'

Caitlin sat a little straighter and pinned a large smile on her face. 'Never off duty, huh?'

'What can I say?' He shrugged. 'It comes with the territory.'

'I'd imagine so.'

Glancing for a second behind him, at the room full of babbling voices, he moved over and sat down beside her. 'So how are you doing?'

'I'm grand. A little tired, just.'

He nodded. 'The lead-up to a wedding can be tiring at the best of times.'

Caitlin studied his profile. 'Are you coming out here to counsel me about marriage?'

'Do you need me to?'

She laughed. 'No, you're okay.'

'I'm glad about that. Some of those talks can take a long time.'

'I'd imagine so.'

They sat in amiable silence for a while. Then Caitlin turned to study his profile. 'You've known Aiden a long time?'

Mike nodded. 'We were in foster care together.'

Her eyes widened slightly in surprise. 'That *is* a long time, then.'

'There's not too many secrets we keep from each other.'

'Except for me.' She added the words he'd left unspoken. It was almost easier now to understand people's reactions to the sudden appearance of a fiancée. It seemed Aiden's friends were no different from her own in that respect.

He smiled at her. 'No, it's true to say that until very recently I knew nothing at all about you. And, having been told everything, I have to say I'm still surprised.'

Her heart caught in her chest as he spoke. Had he guessed? Did he somehow know that their engagement wasn't real?

'You see,' he continued with a smile, 'I hadn't expected him to be the way he is with you.'

'I don't understand, I'm afraid.'

'You're not like anyone he's ever dated before.'

'I'm not?'

Mike laughed at the worried expression on her face. 'Oh, don't worry, Caitlin. That's not a bad thing. He never looked this happy with anyone else.'

'He didn't?'

'No.'

Caitlin tried to unscramble her brain in order to actually add something to the conversation. She still wasn't sure if Mike suspected something. And, truth be told, she wasn't sure she could lie to him if he asked her outright. After all, he might not currently be wearing his collar, but he was a priest nevertheless. And her upbringing wouldn't allow her to tell a lie straight to his face. Even if Aiden could.

But maybe he wasn't trying to question their relationship. Maybe he was just trying to let her know that the relationship he thought they had was a good thing.

'Were they all so very wrong for him?'

Mike shrugged his shoulders. 'I guess so, or he'd still be with one of them.'

Her curiosity got the better of her. 'What were they like?'

'The few I met were all very nice people. But he never looked at any of them the way he looks at you.'

Which meant what, exactly? She frowned slightly as she tried to read between the lines. 'And what way does he look at me?'

'Like you're the most important thing in his life.' Mike's pale eyes locked with hers. 'Some kind of a precious gift he has to take care of. There's nothing fake about the attachment he has to you. I don't think anyone would think there is.'

The words were a double-edged sword.

The part of her that found it easy to sometimes forget that this was all just some game they were playing warmed to the idea that Aiden could look at her that way. Because she wanted him to. They had, in a very short space of time, formed a bond that no one else could possibly understand. Because no one else was living the lie along with them. No matter what happened after the end of the show that bond would always be there.

But the part of her that knew what they were doing was fake—the exact word that Mike had just used—was suddenly uncomfortable sitting beside him. Because although the words could be interpreted as being good—great, in fact, for the grand deception—somewhere in amongst them there was an element of doubt. A small ringing bell that almost seemed to say *I know what this is all about*. And that worried her.

Pinning a smile on her face, she swallowed her doubts and answered, 'Thank you. I really do care about him, Mike.' She knew the words were true the minute they left her mouth. And they surprised her. Though they shouldn't have. She already relied on Aiden being there for her. Maybe more than was actually safe.

'I can see that. And I don't think it matters how you met, Caitlin. Whether it was the internet or not. All that matters is what I see when you look at each other.' He reached out and squeezed her hand, his smile warm. 'I hope you'll hang onto that.'

CHAPTER FOURTEEN

'MIKE came out to have a chat with me earlier. He's a nice guy.'

Aiden rolled towards her in the darkness, a frown on his face. 'What did he say?'

Rolling slightly towards him too, she searched for the blurred image of his face. It had been easier to allow him up onto the bed in her old bedroom a second time. But she was aware of the air tingling between them, of every sound and movement he made. Things were changing between them and she knew it.

'Some nice things about how he's never seen you with anyone the way you are with me. But it was strange.'

'Strange in what way?'

She'd thought about it for most of the tail-end of the night. Even while the rooms of her parents' house had gradually emptied and the last stragglers had made their way home. It was like indigestion. A small ache in her stomach that just wouldn't go away.

'I don't know, Aiden. Strange, just. Like he knew there was something not right about us but was telling me it was okay anyway.'

Aiden mulled over the information and drew Caitlin into his arms without thinking about it. 'What exactly did he say?'

She snuggled in closer and let out a small sigh as she settled in against him. 'He said he's never seen you being with anyone the way you are with me. That there's nothing fake about the way you are with me.'

Again Aiden thought that it might just have been a mistake telling Mike what was going on. But Mike was the one person who knew him inside and out. Maybe he had needed him to say things like that to Caitlin. He stayed silent for several long moments while he thought that over.

But if he could manage to do one thing right amongst all the other lies he could manage at least to be honest about how he felt.

'There isn't anything fake about the way I am when I'm with you.'

Caitlin felt her heart speed up at the softly spoken words.

'And he's right that I've never been this way with anyone else.' He took a breath. 'When all this is over I really think we should talk.'

'You do?' The question barely made it out on an audible level.

'Yes, I do. Because things are just too complicated right now for us to talk about it all.'

He was right. But the very fact that he still wanted to be around to talk when it was all over gave her a surge of hope. 'I thought when this was all over we'd go back to our lives the way they were before. That I'd never see you again.'

He held his breath. 'And is that what you want?'

She pulled herself as close to him as the separating duvet would allow. 'No. It's not.'

Leaning in to find her mouth in the darkness, he kissed her for a long, lingering moment before whispering, 'Honey, it's not what

I want either. I never planned on doing this show to meet someone like you.'

'Me neither.'

'And this is all very fast.'

'I know.'

He kissed her again. 'Everything will get very complicated as we get closer to the wedding.'

She felt a chill run over her bones at the thought of it. 'I know that too. But if we keep being honest with each other then we'll get through this.'

'You believe that now?'

'I do *now*.' She reached a hand up to touch the side of his face, her thumb brushing back and forth against his cheek. 'Because of you. I know I can get through this when you're here. With you beside me tonight everything was—I don't know—easier, I guess. It didn't even feel like we were lying at times. Maybe I should worry about that.'

Aiden felt his heart twist at her words. She had faith in him. A faith he just didn't deserve. 'There's so much I want to tell you—'

'Shh.' She placed her thumb across his mouth. 'Now that I know you still want to be around when all this is over I know we have time. It can wait.'

Before he could say anything more she placed her mouth against his and tangled her fingers in his hair. In an instant there was no need for any more words. Because all the communication they needed was transmitted into the kiss.

Aiden groaned deep in his throat and moved his lips in time with hers, taking what she was giving and offering more in return. This was the most honesty they had. There were no lies, no deceptions, in the need he had for her. He was a drowning man and she was his lifeline.

He removed his arm from her waist. It wasn't needed to pull her closer once she started moving in a sensual horizontal dance. Did she have any idea what moving like that could do to his imagination?

Caitlin swore inwardly at the cumbersome barrier of the duvet. Whose dumb idea had it been that he should lie on a different side of it from her? Because right that second she *really* wanted it gone.

She *desperately* needed it gone as his mouth grew firmer and his hand began to run up along her arm, along her shoulderblade, to flirt with the pulse at the base of her neck.

The room was suddenly very warm.

Moving her mouth at more of an angle to his, she began to feel her neck protest. But her neck's needs ran a very low second to the needs awakening in the rest of her body. Without thinking about it, she rolled slightly so that she was lying on top of him, her body touching all along the length of his. And even the duvet couldn't hide the truth from her.

She smiled as she raised her head, her nose against his like a marker point in the darkness. 'There appears to be something between us.'

Aiden laughed. 'That would be your fault.'

'We could get it out of the way.'

'No, it's not going anywhere right now.' He ran his hands into her short hair, massaging her scalp with his fingertips.

She nudged his nose with hers. 'Afraid to fool around in my parents' house, Aiden?'

Teenage memories of old made that scenario vaguely erotic to his already tortured body. 'Honey, I'll fool around with you any place you want me to.'

'So maybe we should do something about this thing between us.'

'If we do that we may end up doing more than fooling around.'

Caitlin was surprised to discover that the idea wasn't at all unappealing. It had been a long time since she'd felt that way. And she hadn't ever 'fooled around' or anything beyond that in her parents' house since Liam. The realisation that she didn't feel guilty being that way with someone else made her slow down. What was she doing, throwing herself at him like this? She'd never before been tempted to get physically close to someone so fast. And the last thing she wanted Aiden thinking was that she was some kind of slut.

'You know I'm talking about the duvet, right?'

'Of course you are. Me too.'

She could almost feel his smile in the darkness, and she wriggled against him one last time before rolling back into her position at his side. 'Maybe it's just as well it's there.'

'We're still talking about the duvet, right?'

She laughed softly. 'Yes. If it weren't there then we might get carried away.'

And, Lordy did he want to. But he knew that complicating matters that way wouldn't be the best decision he could make. Caitlin already had him upside down.

'And that wouldn't be a good idea in your parents' house?'

'No. They probably wouldn't appreciate it if we kept them up all night with the noise.'

He groaned again. 'Okay, you don't need to say anything more. I'm already way past the point of reason, and you doing the verbal foreplay thing with me isn't helping any.'

Caitlin positively glowed beside him, revelling in the sense of power his words gave her. She was empowered by the knowledge that she could have as much of an effect on him as he had on her. And his being so honest about it made it easier for her to open up in return.

'There's no one at my house to listen, though. If we did decide to fool around some-times…'

Aiden reached his arm around her again and took a breath. 'I think you're only too aware that I'm up for a little fooling around with you. But it wouldn't be a good idea right now, would it?'

'Probably not.'

He squeezed his arm a little tighter when he heard the regret in her voice. It was funny how in the dark it was easier to read the inflections in her voice. Almost as if his senses made up for the lack of sight by simply *feeling* emotions in the air between them.

'There are cameras in your house—cameras that pick up sound. And even if there weren't, honey, I can't make love to you while we're doing this show. There's only so much I can let people see on screen.'

She knew he was right. But suddenly three months seemed an awfully long time.

'I know. You're right. Again.'

He kissed her, then raised his head enough to whisper against her swollen lips, 'But you have to know it's not that I don't want to.'

Her hand ran along the side of his face again as she smiled. 'Me too.'

They remained silent for a while as their hands traced each other's faces in the darkness. Then Aiden whispered again, 'Do something for me?'

'I thought we just agreed that wouldn't be a good idea.'

'*Minx*. I meant something else.'

'Name it, then.'

'When all this is over, remember this stuff. Hang onto it no matter what happens.'

She felt the indigestion sensation return to her stomach. 'Mike said something similar to that.'

Aiden raised an eyebrow. 'He did?'

'Yes, and I had the same bad feeling then that you've just given me now.'

He ran his fingertips in a soothing circle against her temple. 'A lot of things can happen these next few months. Weddings can be traumatic at the best of times.'

'Maybe that's what he meant, then. He's afraid I'll run away before you get me to the altar.'

'Maybe. But we both know that's not going to happen.' He continued trying to soothe her with his touch. 'I'm talking about afterwards, when we've been through all the rough stuff.'

'Like telling the truth?'

'Yes, that kind of thing.'

'It won't be easy, Aiden. I've known that from the start.'

'Then you have to know that when the truth all comes out it may be difficult for us to look at each other.'

She touched her thumb to the edge of his mouth. 'It won't change this, though.'

'No, it won't change this. And that's why I need you to remember.'

'I will.' She leaned in to kiss him again. Softly this time, making the kiss a promise. 'How could I forget?'

Aiden sent a silent plea into the night that she would remember. Because he genuinely hoped that the more of these kind of memories he could place in her heart and her mind, the more chance he might have of her not hating him when everything else was done with.

Because he didn't want to lose her. He was falling in love with Caitlin Rourke.

CHAPTER FIFTEEN

IN THE chaos of the weeks that followed the engagement party it was Izzy who first smelled a rat.

It was when they finally found *the dress*. The one they'd been searching all over Dublin for. Caitlin hadn't thought that she'd want the perfect dress so badly for something that was a big fat lie. But she did. And everything she tried on just wasn't right.

Until a tiny little shop produced the perfect one.

She stood in front of the three large angled mirrors and stared at her reflection with wide eyes while her mother searched for a handkerchief in her handbag.

'Sweetheart, it's perfect.' She sniffed loudly. 'You look just beautiful.'

Caitlin was vaguely aware of Mick moving the camera around to her side for a better angle. But she couldn't look away from the mirrors in front of her.

The dress transformed her. It wasn't just that it was a beautiful cut, or that the material flowed against her skin like the touch of a lover. It wasn't that she didn't love the fact that she looked like the princess every bride should look like.

It was the fact that some time during the search for cakes, flowers and invitations she had allowed herself to get sucked into the fantasy.

Because now that she was looking at herself in the mirror she was imagining Aiden's face as he stood at the top of an aisle, waiting for her. And she wished, for the briefest moment, that it wasn't all a lie.

She was in love with Aiden.

When had it happened? With sudden clarity she realised it had been sneaking up on her for weeks. How could she not have known?

A smiling assistant appeared behind her to pin a floor-length veil to the back of her head and Caitlin continued to stare.

The time had just flown so fast, when she'd thought that it would drag by. That the weight of deceit would slow everything down. But Aiden had been there every single day. He was there in her house every night when she returned from work, and on the days when she had time off. They behaved like a couple. To all intents and purposes they were a couple. They just weren't a couple who were actually getting married or who had met the way everyone thought they had.

It was slightly less of a lie than it would have been if they'd remained disliking each other, as they had in the beginning. But that dislike was long since gone now that she knew him better. In fact, they didn't even bother to hide that fact from the cameras any more. Aiden almost seemed determined to show on film what was happening between them. He'd reasoned to her that there was no way the viewer would think that it was anything more than the part they were both playing. Something that Caitlin had debated with him.

Though it had been hard to argue when she so badly wanted him to touch her and kiss her.

But some time during all the time that they'd spent together she'd started to fall in love with him. And now, standing looking at herself in the mirror, it had finally hit her.

What was she going to do?

She knew that he cared about her, that he wanted them to talk after the show was over. But what if everyone hated them for what they'd done, for using them all for a cash pay-off? How could a relationship overcome that? There was the very real chance that they would have to chose between salvaging the relationships they had with all the other people they cared about and their new relationship that had been founded on a lie.

What if she had to give him up?

It was while that anguish tore through her that her eyes finally locked with Izzy's. And a frown appeared on Izzy's face.

She could see there was something wrong. Even the smile that Caitlin pinned on her face didn't convince her friend.

As they left the shop, purchase made and her mother leaving to look for her own outfit, Izzy turned on her. She searched her face with knowing eyes and then took a breath. 'There's something not right here.'

'You don't like the dress?' Caitlin began to walk along the street, hiding her eyes from her perceptive friend.

'No, I love the dress. Like your mother said, it's perfect. What's not right is how you looked when you saw yourself in it.' A hand on her arm halted Caitlin's movement. 'What's going on, Cait?'

'I'm getting married. That's what's going on. I thought everyone had got that part.'

'Oh, they've got that.' Izzy stood her ground, 'But there's something else, isn't there? Something you're not telling us. Don't you want to marry Aiden?'

That at least she could answer honestly. Even if she had to chose her words carefully. Using *I want to* instead of *I'd love to*. 'Of course I want to marry Aiden.'

'Then why did you just look like your world was coming to an end?'

Caitlin pinned a smile on her face. 'Doesn't everyone get a moment where they worry about the commitment they're about to make?'

'Pre-wedding jitters? Is that what this is?' Izzy didn't look convinced. 'It looked like more than that.'

'It's not.' The lie slipped off the end of her tongue. Maybe this lying thing was getting easier after all.

Izzy studied her as her eyes moved away again. She frowned and squeezed Caitlin's arm. 'Look at me.'

Caitlin took a breath and forced her eyes to look into Izzy's. She raised her chin a notch and blinked at her, her expression controlled. 'What?'

Izzy shook her head. 'There's something, Cait. I can feel it. I know you too well.'

'You're wrong.' Another lie.

Izzy's eyes sparked with anger. 'You've never held back from me before.'

'I'm not now.' And another lie.

'Damn it, Caitlin. Yes, you are!' Her hand dropped as she glanced around them in frustration. 'I've watched you with Aiden since the party, and there's just something not quite right. But then you look at each other a certain way and I think it's all in my head.'

'It is.' The lies just kept on coming. And a part of her was dying with every one. If it came down to it could she chose Aiden over Izzy and her family? Could she really give up one part of her life to try and build another?

Izzy studied her again for what felt like the longest time. Emotions played across her face, from anger to disbelief to disappointment. 'You've changed. I don't know why, but you have. When you're with him it's plain to everyone looking that you're in love with him. But when you're away from him you just get—I don't know—sad, almost.'

Caitlin blinked at her, trying to hold the pain from her face at the truth of Izzy's words. When she was with Aiden it was easy to forget everything else. It was only when she was away from him that the doubts demanded her attention.

'Is it Liam? Is that what it is? Do you feel guilty that you're marrying someone else?'

The fact was that Liam didn't even enter into it any more. And that fact should have made her sad in itself. In falling for Aiden she'd let go of Liam. Something she'd thought she would never be able to do.

'It's not Liam.'

Izzy seemed to recognise the honesty. 'Then what is it?'

She shook her head. 'It's nothing.'

'You're lying to me, Caitlin. I don't know why, but you are.' Izzy stepped back slightly from her. 'I'm your best friend, and it's my job to be here for you. But I can't do that if you can't be honest with me. The fact that I love you means I can't just sit by and let you make a mistake. If that's what this is.'

Caitlin felt Izzy distancing herself from her in more than the steps she took away. And she had a glimpse of how painful it would be to make a choice between the people she loved and the man she loved. She wasn't sure she could do it if this was even half of how bad it would feel. There wouldn't be a choice. Not for her. She'd have to let him go.

'I won't be making a mistake going through with this wedding, Izzy. You have to trust me on this. If you love me.'

Izzy stood still. 'I do love you.'

'Then believe that I'm doing what I have to do.'

A flash of pain crossed Izzy's eyes as she looked at her. 'I feel like I don't know you any more, Caitlin. How did that happen to us?'

Caitlin swallowed hard. 'We'll get over this. I promise you we will. It'll all get better after the wedding.' She searched for words to ease her friend's fears. 'I never wanted a big wedding, Izzy, and I'm finding all this a lot tougher than I thought it would be. Just bear with me and everything will work out the way it's supposed to. Trust me.'

'I'm trying to.' Izzy glanced over her shoulder, getting her emotions under control. 'I really am.'

*   *   *

'Caitlin's not here.'

'I know that. I didn't come to see my daughter.'

Aiden looked into Brendan Rourke's face and realised that the conversation he'd been avoiding had come to Caitlin's front door. 'You'd better come in.'

They moved into the living room and Aiden's eyes automatically strayed to the camera on the wall. He waited until the older man turned to face him, his expression stern.

'I'd like to know why my daughter is marrying you.'

Aiden opened his mouth to speak, only to be interrupted.

'And I don't want some lie about it being all about love. Because there's more to it than that.'

'Why would there be anything else to it?'

'Because Caitlin has never kept secrets from us. Not even when she was a teenager. She's always talked to me. Until *you* came along.'

'We never meant to keep it a secret.' Aiden stuck to the game plan. 'But things just happened very fast. That happens sometimes.'

'And you're getting married in a few weeks rather then waiting because…?'

'Because we want to get married. We don't want to wait.'

'You don't want to wait? Or you're worried she might change her mind before you get her down that aisle?' He folded his arms across his broad chest and dared Aiden to contradict him.

It had been a long time since another man had intimidated Aiden. But Brendan Rourke was an intimidating man. And not just because of his size.

'If you found someone as special as Caitlin would you want to take a chance on letting her go?' He folded his own arms in a similar stance. Whether it was defensive or to show he could be just as determined as the older man, he wasn't quite sure. 'I waited a long time to find her, Mr Rourke. And when we get married we'll both be doing it because we want to. Because we both have something to gain.'

He weighed Aiden's words carefully in his mind before asking bluntly, 'Have you money, Aiden?'

The question caught him off guard. 'If you're asking me whether I can provide for Caitlin, then the answer is yes.'

'No, what I'm asking you is whether she's marrying you *because* you have money.'

Aiden's eyes widened. 'I'm not poor. But I'm not a millionaire either.'

'My daughter has been deliberately vague about what you actually do for a living.'

Probably due to the fact that Aiden himself had been deliberately vague about what he did for a living. She knew he was working on a book of sorts. But not too much more than that. Because when they talked about it he always managed to distract her, one way or another.

'Right now I'm a writer. I'm working on the manuscripts my father left when he died. He'd worked on them his whole life and I'm finishing what he started.'

'And that makes you a living, does it?'

'He also left a house and some money. Like I said, I'm not exactly poor.' And he had a more than average salary in his real job. But it wasn't as if he could mention that, was it?

Brendan continued to study him with cool eyes, then he raised his chin and asked, 'Has she talked to you about my business?'

Aiden's jaw dropped slightly and his eyes flew to the camera again. 'You do know there are cameras in this house?'

'Oh, I'm only too aware of the bloody cameras.' Brendan followed his gaze before looking back at his face. 'And I'm assuming from that answer that she *has* talked to you.'

'Yes, she has.' Aiden sought for words to reassure the older man that his business wasn't becoming public knowledge—and wouldn't if he had any say in it. Which he did. 'But not in front of the cameras. So be careful what you say.'

'I don't give a damn about what's said in front of these cameras. I may be proud, but I'm also human. I make mistakes. And if the people watching this ridiculous show can't respect that fact then frankly I don't care what they think.' He aimed the last words directly at the camera before turning his back on it and adding, 'What I do care about is my daughter. And I won't have her marrying you to help get me out of financial difficulties.'

He was so much closer to the truth than he realised that Aiden had to take a few seconds to unscramble his thoughts. He had a renewed respect for this man. For the fact that he could put his family before his own pride. Caitlin was trying to protect someone at great personal cost, when that person really didn't need anyone to protect him.

'I'm marrying your daughter because I love her. I'll do whatever makes her happy. And if that means helping you out along the way then that's fine with me.' He mixed as much truth into the deception as he could manage. 'Whether or not you accept our help won't change what we're doing.'

'I won't take money from you. You'd better tell my daughter that too. And I won't walk her down the aisle to you if that's why she's doing this.'

'You honestly think that Caitlin would trap herself in a loveless marriage to get you out of trouble?'

His shoulders slumped imperceptibly at the question, 'I would like to hope she'd know better than that. She'd know I'd never allow that to happen.'

'Then you have to believe that there's more to this than just money.'

Brendan seemed to accept that. 'I know that when I see her look at you I see something in her I haven't seen in a long time.'

Aiden felt his heart beat harder at the statement. 'What Caitlin wants matters to me, Mr Rourke. I would never let her do something she didn't want to do. The things she cares about I care about. And what makes her happy makes me happy.'

Brendan took a moment and then seemed to soften, unfolding his arms and looking around the room before he looked back at him. 'That's what loving someone means. You give before you look for anything for yourself.'

'Which is why I understand your wanting to talk to me about all this.'

'All I want is for her to be happy, Aiden. There's nothing in my life more important than that. My family comes first in everything.'

Aiden nodded. 'And that's the way it's supposed to be. I'd have thought less of you if you'd thought any other way.' He unfolded his own arms and took a step closer to him. 'I may not have much experience with a real family, Mr Rourke, but I know how it's meant to be. And I know that what you have is a very precious thing. When this programme goes out I think that's what the world will see.'

'They'll just be seeing things the way they are. What I have in my family is what I'll spend my last breath fighting for.'

'I wish my own father had felt the same way you do.'

Brendan studied Aiden's face as he spoke the simple words and then nodded with renewed respect for the younger man before him. 'He should have. And it was his loss not knowing it. You didn't deserve that. No one does.'

'No, they don't.' Aiden blinked slowly. 'It's a mistake I'll never make with my own family.'

They stared at each other for another long moment, each one taking the time to absorb a new understanding of the other. Then Brendan reached out a large hand to shake Aiden's.

'You'll do, lad.' He smiled a warmer smile. 'But just so you know—I still won't take your money. And if you ever do anything to make my daughter cry, you'll have me to answer to.'

CHAPTER SIXTEEN

SHE stood silently in the doorway, watching him. He was sitting at the dining room table, his laptop in front of him. But he wasn't looking at the screen. He was looking out of the windows to the small dark courtyard beyond. Lost in his thoughts.

Her eyes studied his profile, memorising each detail of him from the curl of his dark hair against the nape of his neck to the line of his strong jaw.

And all the while she drank in the beautiful sight of him, right there in her house and in her life, she was already beginning to mourn the time when he wouldn't be there.

It was a loss that she would have to carry with her for ever. When she'd lost Liam she'd known he was gone. That there would never be a time she'd see him again. Whereas with Aiden she'd have to live her life knowing he was still there. Was breathing, laughing and loving while she was dragging her way through the days without her heart.

When she'd dived headlong into this she'd done it for the best reasons. To give back to her family something that was important to them. But in doing so she'd never thought she would lose something just as important.

His eyes moved and he caught sight of her reflection in the dark glass. He smiled and turned to look at her. 'Hey.'

She smiled back at him. 'Hey.'

'How did the dress-hunt go?'

'It went fine.'

'You got one, then?'

'Yes, I got one.'

'Well, that's another tick off the list.' He continued to smile encouragingly. 'Not much left to do now.'

'No.'

They were on the homeward stretch. Soon it would all be over. She thought of telling him about her conversation with Izzy. But in telling him she'd be giving away a little of what she felt, and she couldn't do that. Not now that she'd made the decision to let him go when it was all over.

She glanced across at the kitchen. 'Did you eat yet?'

'No, I thought I'd wait for you.' He watched as she moved away from the door, studying her face. She was different somehow. Or maybe he was just looking at her differently after his talk with her father. He couldn't tell her what Brendan had said. Because it would kill her to know they were going through all this for nothing. They'd just have to find a way to get him to take the money when it was all over. *Together.* When Brendan knew the whole story surely he'd realise that family meant as much to his daughter as it did to him. He'd have to take it or he'd be making them all unhappy—Caitlin most of all.

'I got your Christmas stuff out. I thought we could put the tree up tonight.'

She had barely even thought about Christmas, despite the ever-current reminders surrounding her in the outside world. Because she'd had more to think about than decorations and presents.

'Okay, that sounds like a plan. I'll throw us together something simple, then.'

'You want some help?' Pushing his chair back, he moved round to join her. 'I'm getting quite good at this kitchen thing now.'

That brought a smile to her face. 'You think?'

Once at her side, her nudged her shoulder with his. 'I haven't burnt anything in days.'

'That's as maybe, but I still think it's safe to say your talents don't lie in the kitchen.'

'No,' He leaned his head towards hers, his voice low. 'I definitely have more talent in other areas.'

Her eyes darkened. 'Indeed you do.' The 'fooling around' thing had been hard to avoid over the last weeks. Sneaking away from the cameras for a few minutes here and there had only served to heighten the sexual tension between them. But she needed to distance herself a little from that kind of heat now. For her own

self-preservation. 'So how is the writing coming along?'

'Pretty much done. Ready for the open
world.' He grimaced slightly at the thought.
But then there was always that initial moment
of doubt before one of his projects went up for
public scrutiny.

'You'll send it to a publisher to look at?'

He nodded. 'It would be a shame for both
my father and I to have spent time on it for it
not to see the light of day. I always intended
for someone to see it.'

Caitlin knew about the project he'd spent
the six months before they'd met working on.
It was why he needed the money from the
show, she guessed. It was his tribute of sorts.
To a man who had never been there for him.
She didn't understand why he felt the need to
do it. But he was passionate about it, and so
that made it worthwhile in her eyes.

'Can I read it?'

Aiden shrugged, trying to make out that it
didn't matter to him one way or another if she
wanted to. The truth was he *did* want her to

read it, to understand some of his reasons behind doing what he'd done in deceiving her. 'If you like.'

'Okay, then. We'll have dinner and then I'll read it while you do the decorations.'

'You want *me* to do the decorations?' He blinked at her in surprise.

Christmas decorations were hardly his forte. All he had was one of those fibre optic things that plugged in and he was done. And the boxes he'd carted down from her attic seemed to hold a million small tinkling items.

'On my own?'

Caitlin laughed at his expression. 'I'll direct from the sofa.'

'Will, you indeed? And what's my reward for all this hard work?'

She held a smile on her face. 'You get to see me in my great dress in a couple of weeks.' Then she glanced away from the intensity in his eyes.

He stared at her, a sudden mental image forming of her walking towards him in a wedding dress. And he swallowed hard. In his imagination the picture wasn't fake. It was real. And it was what he wanted. *All of it.* Caitlin Rourke, her family and her friends, mixing with his own. He'd had a very real glimpse these last few weeks of what it would be like to be a part of her life. And he didn't want to let go of it.

He wanted happily ever after.

In the small hours of the morning the final decorations were put in place and Aiden switched on the lights, transforming the room into a fairy tale. He looked round at the warm room, completed by Caitlin curled on the large sofa, his laptop on her knees.

He smiled. It had been the worst kind of torture, watching her read his work. It had taken huge self-control not to ask what she thought each time she hit the key to scroll down through the pages.

And even more self-control not to walk over and take the laptop from her to pull her close. She was just so beautiful. And all the more so because she was so completely unaware of it.

She was chewing on her bottom lip as she read, a small frown of concentration between her eyes. Every so often a different reaction would flicker across her face, or an occasional gasp could be heard over the soft classical music in the background. He had smiled contentedly as he'd played with the decorations, often having to ask a couple of times before he got an answer to where a given trinket was supposed to live.

'Done.'

She didn't look up from the screen. 'It's lovely.'

He grinned. 'You haven't looked.'

Her eyes glanced up and moved briefly around the room, 'Lovely.' Then she went back to the screen.

Aiden could take no more. He moved across and sat down beside her, waving a hand in front of the screen. 'Hello? Earth calling Caitlin.'

She batted his hand away. 'I'm reading. Go away.'

He moved his hand to beneath her thigh and gently kneaded her skin through her soft jeans. 'I have nothing to do now.'

'Well, go make a cup of tea or something, then.'

She hadn't looked up but he saw the soft flush touch her cheeks and knew she wasn't immune to his touch. 'I don't want tea.'

Caitlin tried hard to ignore where his hand was and concentrate on the words on the screen. But it was a lost cause. She looked up at him with blinking eyes. 'You didn't tell me.'

He raised an eyebrow. 'That I didn't want tea?'

'No, you idiot. That this was so wonderful.' She stared into his eyes. 'This isn't just a history story. You said your father was a historian.'

'He was.'

'But this isn't just local history. It's dozens of love stories from one generation to the next, all wrapped up in the history of each of those times.'

He nodded. 'I ad-libbed some.'

She leaned towards him, a look of wonder on her face. 'This isn't just a book either. It's a film on paper.'

His eyes avoided hers as he removed the laptop from her knees. 'You think so?'

'Yes, I do.' She changed position so that her legs rested over his and she was closer to his side. 'It's like I can see each scene in front of my eyes as I read it. You should try to do something with this. Maybe some of the people from this show could help you.'

'Maybe.' He made a show of shutting the laptop down and closing it. 'I'm glad you liked it.'

Lifting a hand, she touched his chin and drew his face around towards hers. 'It's wonderful.' She smiled at him, her eyes sparkling in the firelight. 'Do you have any idea how talented you are?'

Twining his fingers with hers against his face, he looked deep into her eyes, his voice filled with emotion. 'It's not all my work, honey. I just added to it, that's all. This is what my father left behind.'

Searching his eyes, she slowly began to understand. 'It must have taken years for him to put all the details together. Hundreds of years of history.'

Aiden nodded. 'Yes.'

'And he had to have been driven to complete it.'

He removed their joined hands from his face and looked down at them. 'Yes.'

Her voice shook. 'So driven that he shut everything else out, didn't he? Even you.'

He couldn't look at her.

Caitlin squeezed his fingers tight. 'And you understood that when you started to read what he'd done. This is your way of showing you forgive him.'

Aiden continued to study their hands as he bared his soul for the first time. He cleared his throat for good measure. 'I couldn't have done what he did. I would never have been driven enough to give up the people I loved.'

Tears formed in Caitlin's eyes as she listened to the husky edge in his voice.

'So, no, I don't forgive him. I don't know that I ever will. But I understand. And doing this is the best way I knew to show that. Someone should know what he gave up his life to tell.'

'You filled in the blanks.' She tugged at his hand until he looked at her. 'You put in the love that he had left out while he did this. *You* did that.'

Reaching out his free hand, he brushed the tears from her face as he smiled sadly. 'Don't cry. It's all right. I had to do this and now it's done. And it was worth the heartache of doing it if it brought me to you.'

I love you. The words were on the edge of her tongue. How could she not love him? This strong, silent man who was clearing away the demons of his past by making his own personal tribute to the man who had caused those demons in the first place.

They both had their own reasons for doing the show. But each of those reasons was deeply seated in love for family. One family that lived in love and one that had lived without.

But in making that realisation in her own heart Caitlin was made all the more aware of what she was going to have to give up.

If they'd just met some other way. If she'd seen him on the street, or been introduced at some stupid party. Would she even have given him the chance to get this close?

She'd been carrying demons of her own. Demons attached to the love she'd had and lost. She'd never believed that she could love someone more than she'd loved Liam. But she'd been a child then. And now she was a woman. And the woman loved this man with all she had.

She detached her hand from his to wrap her arms around his neck and draw herself close, until her head was hidden against his shoulder.

There had to be a way. She had to find a way to make her family and friends see that even though she'd deceived them all she wasn't actually lying. They had to understand. Because she couldn't give him up.

But either way. Whether she chose him or them. She was headed into heartbreak.

There *had* to be a way.

CHAPTER SEVENTEEN

HER eyes narrowed as she studied Cara and Izzy, deep in conversation on the patio. Her bridesmaids were wrapped in several layers of clothes to withstand the cold as Cara had a cigarette outside. And every so often their eyes would stray towards the house and then look away.

Whatever it was that was bugging Izzy so much was obviously fuel to add to Cara's fire too.

'You okay?' Aiden's hand touched the small of her back as he reached her side. 'You look tired.'

She was tired. Exhausted, in fact. Emotionally and physically. It was only a couple of days until the 'wedding', and she had the weight of the world on her shoulders.

Not only was she about to face up to her family, she was also about to make a choice that would stay with her for the rest of her life. And having a decision like that to make wasn't exactly conducive to a good night's sleep.

Plus, her mother had insisted they go through the tradition of wedding party nights. When all their friends and family would come to the house to bring presents and wish the happy couple well over drinks.

'Izzy and Cara are up to something.'

Aiden's eyes were drawn to the patio. 'You think they're trying to plan a hen night after all?'

Caitlin might have given in on all the other wedding traditions that her family had insisted on, but she'd drawn the line at a drunken night of carousing with her friends. The last thing she needed at this stage was to get drunk on top of her present exhaustive state. Who knew what she would end up blurting out?

'No, I don't think it's that. I think Izzy knows something.'

His eyes widened slightly at the words he had to lean closer to hear. 'What makes you think that?'

Caitlin sighed. 'She pulled me about it the day I got my dress.'

'Why didn't you tell me?'

'Because she didn't mention it again.' And she hadn't. On any of the occasions they'd been together. Through dress-fittings and hairdresser consultations and shopping for shoes, she hadn't said a word about it. But she'd been withdrawn, had kept Caitlin at arm's length, so that she knew it still wasn't right between them.

'And you think she's talking about it with Cara now?'

Caitlin nodded. 'Cara hasn't exactly been a big fan of you and me from the beginning.'

They were so close to it all being over. Aiden wasn't about to let anyone stop it now. He needed this thing finished so he could get things out in the open. So they could start again, without any lies between them.

'I'll talk to them.' He moved towards the doors.

Caitlin stopped him with a hand on his. 'No.' She smiled up at him with weary eyes.

'I will. They're my responsibility. You stay here and talk to the people that just came in.'

He seemed to hesitate for a moment, and Caitlin prepared herself for a debate on the subject. But then he smiled and leaned down to brush a kiss across her mouth. 'Here's hoping they didn't bring a sandwich-maker.'

She smiled. They already had four to return when all this was over. And a roomful of varying household appliances. Everyone had been so great. It made her feel like pond scum.

The conversation came to a grinding halt when she opened the door. 'What are you two talking about? It all looks very cloak and dagger.'

They both stared at her as she smiled at them from the open doorway,

'There's no chance I can get you to come in where it's warmer, is there?'

'No, we're grand here.' Izzy folded her arms across her chest.

Caitlin shrugged and wished she'd stopped for a coat. 'Fine, then. I'll just come out here.' She closed the door.

'You'll freeze.' Cara stated the obvious. 'Can't have you all red-nosed on the big day, now, can we?'

Caitlin recognised sarcasm when she heard it. 'Okay. Out with it, then.'

They looked at each other. Then Izzy looked her straight in the eye. 'Are you going to tell us what's going on?'

'I'm getting married. Day after tomorrow.'

'To someone you've barely known five minutes.' Cara glared at her.

'Who you don't happen to like.' She stood her ground, fighting off the chill the cold air brought to her body. 'And that's your loss, by the way. He's the most incredible person I've ever met.'

'Well, we've all known for years you needed to get out more.'

'Maybe you're right. Maybe I should have gone out more after Liam died. But I wasn't ready, and that's the truth of it. I met Aiden at the right time. It doesn't matter how that happened or how fast.'

Izzy blinked at her. 'If you're so crazy about him then how come you're so bloody sad before you marry him?'

Caitlin stared straight at her. 'Maybe it's because two of the people I care most about won't accept the fact that I'm in love with him!'

There was a split moment of stony silence and then Cara's voice sounded. 'That's the first time you've said that to us. *To any of us.* Did you know that?'

Was it? She searched back through the chaos to the things that she'd said to them all. The reasons she'd given for this wedding. They were right. She'd never said it before. Maybe she hadn't been able to lie about something that important. And until very recently it would have been the biggest lie of all.

Now it wasn't a lie.

'I love him. More than I could ever try to explain to any of you.' Her voice cracked on the words that she'd been so desperate to say out loud—to *someone*. Just so she could let it out. 'And whether or not you think there's something else going on is up to you. I can't make up your minds for you.'

'But there *is* something else, isn't there?' Izzy moved towards her, her arms unfolding and concern showing in her eyes. 'Something else you don't think you can tell us.'

Cara stood too, and stepped closer, her voice soothing. 'You can tell us anything.'

A sob broke from Caitlin's throat. 'Not this time.'

Izzy opened her mouth to speak. But Caitlin held a hand up in front of her.

'No, Izzy. Not this time. You can both think what you want. But I know what I'm doing.' She looked over at her sister. 'I love him. And I'm going ahead with this wedding. Nothing will change that. Whether or not you both want to be there to support me is up to you.'

They watched as she turned on her heel, then stopped, her hand on the door. She turned around slowly and took a breath before looking at them. 'Please don't make me choose between him and you.'

Then, before they could answer, she turned away from their shocked faces and went back into the house.

She remained silent the whole way back to Dublin. Staring out of the side window while Aiden drove.

Eventually the guys in the back gave up and turned off the camera.

Only when they were back inside the walls of the house, the crew gone, did Aiden reach out for her, his hand capturing hers. 'What is it?'

She smiled sadly up at him. 'Not now, Aiden. I think I'm all talked out for tonight.'

'You had an argument with them?'

She nodded. 'Yes, I did.'

He held onto her hand when she tried to pull away from him. 'What did they say to you?'

'It doesn't matter. Not now. We only have to get through one more day and then this will be over.'

He felt a chill cross his spine. 'No more lies.'

'No more lies.'

Her tone was deadpan, flat. As if they were about to attend a funeral rather than a wedding. And all Aiden wanted to do was pull her close and tell her it would be all right. But he couldn't do that. Because he still didn't know if it would be.

His question came out in a low tone. 'Do you regret doing this, Caitlin Rourke?'

Did she? If she had to go back and do it all over again, would she? Caitlin didn't know the answer to that. She'd been safe before. More lonely than she would probably have allowed herself to admit. But she'd had the love and respect of her family and friends. She'd have had to stand by and watch her father lose everything he'd spent his whole life working for, but she'd still have had his love and respect.

If she hadn't done it would she ever have met Aiden? That would have been left to the fates. There were no guarantees. But surely if she loved him as much as she did now then it was meant to happen? To feel the strongest emotion she'd ever felt before was an amazing experience. And even if he didn't feel the same strength of emotion she wouldn't trade having experienced it. Because now she knew what her heart was capable of feeling.

Turning towards him, she looked into his ridiculously blue eyes and smiled, not caring what he could see in her own eyes. 'I don't regret meeting you. I won't ever forget that.'

He felt as if he couldn't breathe. He looked down into her dark eyes and didn't want to stop looking. Because he'd never seen warmth like that before.

But her words had chilled him again. It was as if she was saying goodbye to him.

'And I won't ever regret knowing you. You have to know that.'

She continued smiling. 'I do know. I just wish sometimes that we'd met some other way.'

'Me too.'

Letting go of her hand, he reached both hands up to frame her face, his thumbs moving across her cheeks and his fingertips into her short hair. He wanted to freeze the moment, to not put them through what was coming. But he knew they had to go through it. He had to take a chance and hope that she had got to know him well enough to believe that he hadn't been faking with her.

She reached her hands up and placed them on his forearms, her bottom lip quivering as she tried to continue smiling at him. 'This is our last night in this house.'

He knew that. Had been painfully aware of it all day. 'We could defy tradition and stay here tomorrow night?'

'My mother would have a fit.' Her smile wavered. 'It's bad luck.'

Even he could do without any of *that*. 'Then this is our last night.'

Her eyes darkened and he read their silent message. He wanted it too. Leaning his head down, he kissed her tenderly, his mouth moving softly across hers. He felt her sigh against his lips as he lifted his head again.

Looking down into her eyes, his mouth still inches from hers, he slowly shook his head and whispered, 'I can't.'

She whispered back, 'You don't want to?'

'I do want to. But I can't.'

Caitlin suddenly didn't care any more what the damn cameras picked up. She'd long since given up pretending when she was alone with him. She opened her mouth to tell him why she didn't care, but he silenced her with another long kiss.

He then lifted his mouth and placed it beside her ear, kissing her on the sensitive skin of her neck before whispering, 'I can't make love to you when we're still surrounded by lies.'

Her eyes welled. She understood his reasoning, his sense of honour. But what she felt was real, and she knew him well enough to know he'd been honest with her all along. There weren't any lies when they were alone. She believed that.

But she was very afraid. Afraid that after the wedding things would pull them in different directions. That they might get pulled apart by circumstances. And she wanted the memory of one night with him to hold onto. To bind him to her.

'I'm scared I'll lose you.'

He was scared of the same thing. There was only one way he could think of to try and show her that what they had was real, not some lie that he'd sucked her into. Even as he held onto her he knew that words wouldn't be enough to make up for what he'd held back from her.

If he stayed with her he might not be able to resist the temptation of holding her all night. And holding her all night would only lead in one direction.

He couldn't do that until she knew everything. Until he'd made this thing right again for her. Because even if she forgave him his lies and still wanted him, he couldn't take the chance that she might have to choose between him and everyone else who cared about her. He would walk away before he'd ever let that happen.

And he didn't want to walk away. Not now that he knew there was a Caitlin Rourke in the world.

There was only one thing he could do.

He pulled back from her to look into her eyes. 'You'll never lose me, honey. I'll always be here, for as long as you want me to be. It's always your choice. I want you to remember that. *Promise me.*'

Caitlin frowned slightly in confusion at the determination on his face. 'Aiden, I don't un-der—'

'Promise me.'

She blinked up at him. 'I promise.'

He stepped away from her, releasing her from his touch. 'I have to go.'

'Go where?' She stepped towards him.

'I have someplace I need to be.' He smiled wryly. 'And I can't guarantee that if I stay I won't give in to you.'

Caitlin shook her head. 'But where are you going? Can't you tell me?'

'No.' He shook his head, his hand reaching out to the doorknob behind him. 'Not this time. I just have to go.'

He continued looking at her as he opened the door and a blast of cold air hit his back.

He took a step back. Then stopped and moved forward to kiss her again.

She clung to him, not wanting to let go. It felt as if they were saying goodbye, and she couldn't bear that. She had been ready to have her heart broken one way or another in a day's time, but not right now at this minute.

Their mouths moved in a frenzy, their hands touching each other frantically, and then Aiden dragged himself from her. 'Remember your promise, Caitlin Rourke. Don't forget.'

'I won't forget.'

And then he was gone.

CHAPTER EIGHTEEN

AIDEN wasn't overly surprised to find Aisling in the editing room. Her eyes widened when he opened the door.

'What the hell are you doing here?'

'Checking up that you still have no life outside of this place. What else?'

She frowned as he pulled up an office chair beside her and studied the screens in front of him. 'Correct me if I'm wrong but don't you have something to do in just over a day from now? I would have thought that would keep you out of my hair for a while.'

He smiled. 'That's kind of why I'm here.' He set two plastic cups on the console in front of them. 'I even brought coffee.'

Aisling's eyes narrowed as she reached for a cup and carefully removed its lid. 'You only bring coffee if we're about to pull an all-nighter.'

'You've been working for me too long.'

'Yeah, and I'm due a pay rise too.'

'You should put that in writing.'

'Aiden, you never *read* anything I put in writing.' She blew on the top of her coffee cup before sipping cautiously at its contents. 'So what are we doing?'

'Are these the dailies you're looking at?' He looked at a frozen picture on the screen, recognising Izzy in some kind of shop.

'Yes. I got sick of watching the news.'

'Good. Where are the rest of them?'

'*All* of them?' Her eyes widened again. 'Right from the start?'

'Yep.' He smiled a winning smile at her. 'Every second of them.'

'You know how much footage that is, right?'

'I could probably work it out if you got me a pen and some paper, but I have a fair idea that there's an hour or twos worth,' He swung his chair back and forth. 'You've been going through them, though. So they're all in chronological order of some kind.'

She stared at him, wanting badly to stop his damned chair from moving. It had a creak that grated on her nerves. 'I've been putting it together the way we agreed. And I have some of the voice-overs done. But it's far from ready.'

'We're going to redo it all.'

Her coffee went down the wrong way and she coughed for a few seconds before composing herself. 'Sorry—I thought you said we were redoing it all.'

'We are.' He stopped the movement of his chair and leaned towards her, his forearms resting on his jean-clad thighs. 'I need your help.'

'Aiden, it'll take weeks to go through every second of that footage and redo it! And we haven't got Rick booked for another voice-over session 'til next Thursday.' She leaned towards him, her eyes sincere. 'When do you want this done for?'

He smiled slowly, one dark eyebrow quirking. 'The wedding.'

She gaped. 'You've lost the plot!'

'That's just it. I think I just found it.' He reached for her free hand. 'I really need your help.'

'Why?'

'Because it's the only way I can think of to fix this thing.'

She shook her head in confusion. 'Fix what?'

His eyes blinked a couple of times and then he smiled slowly. 'I'm in love with Caitlin Rourke.'

'Oh, well, there's a newsflash.' She grinned. 'Like I haven't been stuck in this room looking at that little piece of information for weeks now. You wouldn't even need subtitles for it. We could just show a close-up of that expression you get when you look at her.'

He continued smiling.

Aisling squeezed his hand before releasing it. She raised her eyebrows. 'Do you have *any* idea of the tricky piece of editing I've had to do to disguise that fact from the public?'

'That's just the thing, Aisling. I don't want to disguise it. I want them all to see. Especially Caitlin.'

'You do?'

He nodded. 'Yes. Because when I tell her my part in all this I'm worried she won't forgive me.'

'Shut up. She's as nuts on you as you are on her.'

He shook his head. 'No, if she's nuts on anyone then it's the person she *thinks* I am. And that's not the whole story.'

'You think she'll go crazy when she finds out you were supposed to make things tougher for her, not easier? That she'll see it as some kind of betrayal?'

'Exactly.'

Aisling started to put it together. 'You think that on top of the stuff she's going to have to confess to her family that'll be the straw that broke the camel's back?'

'Yes.'

She sat back in her chair. 'Oh, my God. You could just be right about that.'

Aiden swallowed hard, taking a moment to control his voice. 'I can't lose her like that. I need back-up.'

The penny dropped and Aisling's face broke into an animated smile. 'Holy cow, Aiden, you need visual evidence!'

'Now you're with me.' He looked up into her eyes. 'I need to be able to show her that what we feel is real. I need them all to see that, so I stand a chance of holding onto her without her losing any of her family or friends as a result of all this.'

Aisling's mind was already spinning with possibilities. 'There's tons of stuff we can use. It's been like watching a bloody love story.'

He laughed, the sound filling the small booth. 'That's exactly what it is. A love story. But it's not just about how I feel or what I hope Caitlin feels too. It's about all kinds of love—love in a family, the lack of love in another family, the love of friends.'

She stared at him again. 'We can do this.'

'But we haven't got a lot of time.'

'Then we'd better get going.' She was already on the case. 'I already know what reels most of the good stuff is on. I'll dig them out and you can go through them. Then we'll call

Rick first thing in the morning and get him in here.'

Aiden was already removing his jacket and rolling up his sleeves.

'You need to ring Mick and get today's stuff in, and we'll need to get the stuff off the remote cameras in Caitlin's house.' She was leaving the room as she shouted back over one shoulder. 'And there's no way you've brought enough damn coffee!'

The house felt like a ghost ship the next morning.

Caitlin wandered aimlessly from room to room, her eyes taking in the Christmas decorations, their lights off, the laptop lying on the kitchen table, Aiden's room with the bed still made. And it was like seeing what her life would be like without him in it.

She spent nearly half an hour sitting on the end of his bed, staring into space. Then she spent twenty minutes crying under the jets of a shower. She made toast and then let it go cold while she stared at the dining room chair where he had sat to write. Then she walked into the living room, where she could still hear his voice as he asked where Tinkerbell lived on the tree.

When the phone rang she almost broke her neck getting to it. 'Aiden?'

'No, it's me. Izzy.'

Caitlin swallowed hard and tried to hold the emotion out of her voice. 'Hi.'

'You okay?'

'Yeah, I'm fine. You?'

'Well, apart from feeling like dirt for not being there for my best friend when she needs me, I'm grand.'

Caitlin went silent and blinked back a fresh wave of tears.

'You still there?'

'Yes.'

Izzy sighed on the other end of the line. 'I still think there's something not quite right here, Cait. I'm not going to lie to you about that. I couldn't.'

She felt a wave of guilt flood over her.

'But what you said last night was very real. You love Aiden, and I know that now. I'd still like to walk up that aisle with you tomorrow, if you'll let me.'

'Of course I'll let you, you idiot.' Her voice wavered. 'I couldn't do it without you. And anyway…'

'Yes?' Izzy's voice was as wobbly as Caitlin's was.

'It's too late to get anyone else to fit in your dress.'

Her doorbell sounded and her heart jumped. 'I've got to go, Izzy. Aiden's here.'

'Okay. I'll see you later, at your parents' place.'

'I'll see you then.' She paused for the briefest second. 'I love you, Izzy.'

'Love you too, sweetie.'

The large smile on her face faded as she opened the door to find Mick and Joe in front of her.

'Don't look so pleased to see us, now.'

'I'm sorry, guys.' She glanced past them to the empty pavement. 'I thought you might have been someone else.'

'No, we haven't seen Aiden since last night.' Joe rubbed his ribs when Mick nudged him. 'When we left you guys here.'

Caitlin frowned at them. 'You don't know where he is?'

They both blinked and shook their heads.

'Can't you ring the other crew to find out?'

'No. Sorry, Caitlin.' Mick's face flushed slightly at her question. 'We're not allowed to have our phones turned on when we're filming. We won't see Lou or John 'til we turn in our reels tonight.'

Her head dropped in disappointment. Where was he?

'Ah, now.' Joe's voice piped up from in front of her. 'I'm sure you'll hear from him before the day is out.'

'I'd better.' She forced the words out from behind clenched teeth as she stood back to allow them into the house. Where in *hell* was he?

He was emotionally drained. He'd been watching and piecing together footage for over twelve hours. And it had been like living it all over again.

Aisling silently placed another cup of coffee in front of him and squeezed his shoulder before leaving the room. Aiden kept on watching.

He'd been right about how amazing Caitlin would look on screen. She was stunning. Her eyes were darker, her skin glowing. Even in close up she was beautiful, and he was just mesmerised by her.

And he'd missed so much that the cameras had caught.

The footage from when they'd first met had made him laugh. Man, he'd looked like hell. Any wonder she'd taken such an instant dislike to him. Then he'd listened to their first conversation across the hall in the darkness, the camera's night vision making everything a pale shade of green as their voices bounced back and forth. He'd heard the flat tone in her voice as she'd told him about Liam for the first time, and he'd remembered how he'd felt when she told him.

So much had happened since then. Had it really only been three months?

Then he'd watched what he hadn't seen, when Mick and Joe had spent their first day with her. He'd listened to the conversation in the car, when she'd talked about how much she missed Liam, what it had been like to lose someone who meant so much. And he'd wanted to reach out into the screen to touch her, to let her know he was there for her.

There was their first argument: shots of him outside her door, trying to get her to talk to him.

Every second was caught. Even conversations he'd thought hadn't been heard. And he was glad that it was him putting it all together, not someone who hadn't lived through it all or felt the emotion attached to it.

Aisling reappeared as he was transfixed with footage of Caitlin's conversation with her mother and Cara after he'd left on the reception booking day. He could understand now why she'd been upset enough to quit.

Especially when he heard her mother say how Liam was probably smiling down on her.

'You need to call Caitlin before she phones the police to look for you.'

He frowned. 'What time is it?' He glanced down at his watch. It was after lunch. She'd already have left for her parents' house. He'd wanted to see her before then, to reassure her again. 'Damn. We're running out of time, here.'

'We'll make it.' Aisling smiled down at him. 'Rick's on his way in for the voice-overs. You finished them yet?'

'Almost.' He ran his hand back through his hair, then down over the stubble on his face. 'We're going to need to pull another all-nighter, aren't we?'

'Probably.' She sighed in resignation. 'But you need to get at least some sleep, or you're going to look like hell at the wedding.'

'This has to be right.'

'And it will be.' She squeezed his shoulder again. 'Now, go call Caitlin and let her know you haven't run out on her.'

He smiled at the irony of the words. Running out on her was the last thing he was doing. Far from it. He was trying his best to stay. He just hoped it would be enough.

CHAPTER NINETEEN

CAITLIN was a walking zombie. A *going to kill Aiden when she saw him* zombie. But in the zombie realm nevertheless.

She'd barely slept. Something she regretted when she was forced to look in a mirror on the morning of her wedding. With her toothbrush sticking out of one corner of her mouth, she stared at her own face and groaned. She looked like hell. It wasn't the way a bride was supposed to look, was it? She sincerely hoped that all the lotions and potions she owned would be true to their wrinkle-removing, bag-decreasing, skin-firming promises.

The night before was supposed to have been a quiet, relaxing time, with her family and those closest to her. It was a night she'd known would test her resolve at this stage, but the unexpected arrival of an estate agent to value the house had knocked her into a state of panic.

Oh, her mother had been very apologetic about it. The woman had apparently been busy for the rest of the week and it was the only slot she'd had to visit them. She'd even apologised profusely for interrupting them. Caitlin had barely managed to be civil to her. And she'd almost given everything away when she'd tried to persuade her mother that they didn't need to sell the house.

And all the while she'd wanted Aiden. Had hated him for not being there. Because one five-minute call halfway through the day hadn't eased the sense of fear that had fallen on her as the day progressed.

'I'm still here,' he had said. But he wasn't, was he? And Caitlin hadn't the faintest idea of what was going on. It had led her to a night full of dreams of a horrific wedding with a bride who couldn't stop crying when there was no groom to be seen at the top of the longest of aisles.

At breakfast everyone put her silence down to nerves. And they weren't entirely wrong about that.

Izzy brought her her first glass of champagne just after ten. 'You look like you need a few of these.'

Caitlin's stomach turned at the thought. 'Is there a Valium in there?'

She laughed. 'No. You want me to get one?'

Yes. 'No, maybe not.' She needed her wits about her, 'Has Aiden rung?'

Izzy's eyes searched her face for several long moments. She seemed to think about asking a question, her mouth opening in preparation, then she shook her head and smiled. 'No. Are you afraid he'll stand you up?'

Caitlin knew it was meant as a joke, to lift her spirits, but it was a tad too close to the dreams that had kept her awake, 'Don't even joke about that.'

'He'll be there. I'd bet my life on it.' Izzy stepped closer to drag Caitlin into a bear hug. 'Now, pin a smile on that face and down that champagne. We're leaving for the hotel in ten minutes.'

So soon? Her stomach rebelled and she pulled out of Izzy's embrace. 'I think I need to be sick.'

Two hands lifted to rest on her shoulders. 'No, you don't. You'll be fine. In two hours you'll be saying ''I do's'', and then the fun really starts.'

Caitlin's tortured eyes glanced over Izzy's shoulder and straight into Mick's camera lens. She smiled weakly. Two hours. Two hours and the 'I do's would be said. And then the 'fun' would definitely start.

'Are we set?'

Aisling looked into Aiden's eyes and smiled. 'We're good to go, boss.'

'You're sure?'

She laughed at his expression. Aiden was usually the one who kept the team together. The one always cool under pressure. Nothing usually fazed him. Funny thing, this falling in love game.

She reached out and patted his cheek. 'Positive.'

He smiled slightly. 'Now you're humouring me, aren't you? It makes me nervous when you do that.'

Stepping back from him, Aisling moved her critical eyes over him from top to toe and back again. She even managed to keep a serious expression on her face as he moved from one foot to the other. 'Well, I have to say it. You don't scrub up too bad for someone who's slept less than five hours in the last forty-eight.'

'Thirty-six.' He tugged at his tie. 'But who's counting?'

She waved a hand. 'Who needs sleep anyway? It's just wasted time.' Then her eyes fixed on his and she smiled again. 'You've done something really amazing with that footage, Aiden. It's a winner.'

God, but he hoped so. It had to be. He opened his mouth to say as much, and then saw Izzy walking towards the stairs. 'Excuse me a second.' His feet propelled him in her direction. 'Izzy?'

One foot already on the bottom step of the sweeping staircase, Izzy looked over her shoulder and frowned. She turned around as he got closer. 'You decided to turn up, then? I guess we should be thankful for that much.'

Aiden's eyebrows shot upward at the sharp tone to her voice. 'You thought I wouldn't?'

'You'd be a dead man if I'd thought that.' She stepped closer and poked him in the chest with one long nail. 'But I have a bride upstairs who has just spent the last twenty minutes throwing up in the bathroom. Where in hell have you been?'

His eyes looked past her and up the stairs, as if he might actually catch a glimpse of Caitlin there. He'd known she would be nervous—but *ill*? He stepped forward, needing to see she was all right.

'Oh, no, you don't.' The long finger became a palm that held him back. 'You can't see her before the ceremony.'

'You said she was sick.'

'She's nervous about doing this with all those people there, that's all.' Izzy frowned up at him. 'A phone call to reassure her wouldn't have gone amiss.'

The simple fact was he'd slept through his alarm. Not surprising, considering the time he'd finally gone to bed and how long he'd done without sleep before that. But waking half an hour after he'd planned had left him running around like a demented man in order to be here in time to make sure everything and everyone was where they should be. Given an extra sixty seconds, he'd probably have felt like throwing up himself.

'I just need five minutes to talk to her.' He sidestepped her hand and took the stairs two at a time.

'Aiden—come back here!' Izzy followed in hot pursuit.

As he hit the first-floor landing it occurred to him that he didn't know what room she was in. So he did the only thing he could. 'Caitlin! Caitlin—where are you?' He continued down the hallway. 'Caitlin Rourke!'

A door opened a few steps from him and Cara's head appeared. Her eyes widened. 'What are you doing?'

'Is Caitlin in there?' He didn't need an answer as Caitlin's voice sounded out from behind the half-open door.

'Is that Aiden?'

'It's me. I'm here.'

'That's good to know. I was beginning to wonder.'

He smiled and tried to get past Cara. Cara, in turn, did her best impersonation of a brick wall. 'Oh, no, you don't.'

'Cara…' his voice lowered '…please don't make me move you.'

Cara raised an eyebrow in a manner only too familiar to him. They weren't so unalike, Caitlin and her younger sister. 'You could *try*.'

He tried charm instead, smiling a smile that brought his dimples out. 'I just need a few minutes. *Please?*'

'Uh-uh.' She shook her head. 'Not happening. My mother would have a fit. It's bad luck.'

'I think we make our own luck.'

'I tried telling him.' Izzy squeezed past and stood next to Cara.

Her movement pushed the door a little wider and Aiden's eyes were immediately drawn to the pale face in the room beyond. His breath caught. 'Hey.'

Caitlin smiled back at him weakly. 'Hey.'

'Izzy said you were sick.'

'I'm just nervous, I guess. It's natural, considering…'

'Considering your twerp of a fiancé did a disappearing act twenty-four hours before your wedding,' Cara mumbled beneath her breath.

'You could have just phoned her this morning.' Izzy folded her arms across her chest. 'Instead of bringing all this bad luck to the door.'

Aiden frowned, but his eyes stayed focussed on Caitlin. 'I slept in. I was going to call this morning.'

'You *slept in*?' Izzy looked outraged. 'On your wedding day?'

His focus was brought momentarily to her wide eyes. 'I had work to do! It was important, and I didn't sleep much.'

'More important than your wedding? Than Caitlin?' Cara's words drew his attention to her. 'That better not be a sign of things to come. Do you have any idea how tense she's been?'

He opened his mouth.

'Was it your book?' Caitlin moved towards the door. 'Did you get someone to look at it?'

His eyes met hers and he continued frowning as he tried to find a truth within the lie that he could actually tell her. 'It's going to be on TV.'

Her eyes lit up. 'That's wonderful. I told you so.'

The smile on her face brought one to his in reply. But the soft tones of her words were still lacking in something. As if a part of her was dying.

'Yes, you did. You have to know there was an important reason, *really important*, to keep me away. Especially now.' His words pleaded for her to understand, to have faith for just a little longer.

'I do know that.' She smiled into his concerned eyes. 'I'll be fine. Really. I just needed to see you.'

'Well, you've seen him now.' Izzy threw the words over her shoulder. 'You'd just better hope your mother doesn't find out that—'

'Aiden!' There was the sound of a stern voice from further down the hall. 'You'd better not be looking at Caitlin. It's bad luck!'

The three sets of eyes at the doorway all looked at the rapidly approaching figure of Maggie Rourke. Izzy nudged Cara hard in the ribs and they both moved forward to pull the door behind them. 'He can't see her. They were just talking through the door.'

Aiden nodded in agreement.

'Well, you can just go away now, then.' She reached them with a frown on her face. 'There'll be no bad luck at this wedding.'

Stepping back from the now closed door, Aiden smiled. 'I'm going, I'm going. I just needed to talk to her.'

'You'll have plenty of time to talk to her after the ceremony.'

He sincerely hoped so.

CHAPTER TWENTY

IT OCCURRED to Aiden, as he waited at the top of the aisle, that weddings weren't that unlike a stage production. There were leading players, an audience, and an elaborate set. But he'd never produced anything before that would have such an impact on his own life.

His palms had long since started to go clammy, and he wiped them along the edges of his dress trousers while his heart beat hard against his chest.

Then an Irish harp played its first chords and he turned around and looked at Caitlin, walking slowly towards him.

In a room packed with people, a sea of faces that seemed to fade around him, he could see only her. That was how it was supposed to be when it was for real, wasn't it?

Except if it was for real the bride would look radiant. Not as if she was walking to her own execution. Even her steps were stilted, her whole frame tense. Her eyes flickered around at the people on either side of the aisle; her throat moved as she swallowed. And when she finally turned her eyes to meet his he could see the anguish there and his heart tore.

What had he been thinking when he'd created all this? Who was he to play with people's emotions? In a way it would be just retribution if she walked away from him and never looked back...

Caitlin, meanwhile, had to force herself to take every forward step. The hand holding her bouquet was shaking, and her breathing was choppy as her heart tried to thud its way out of her chest. This was it, then. In a few minutes Aiden would say his 'I do' after hers, and then she would have to face these people and tell them it was all a lie.

She glanced around at them all, memorising their rapt expressions at the sight of the bride taking her steps towards the man she supposedly loved. And then her eyes moved to Aiden, and her heart twisted so painfully that she almost couldn't breathe.

The man she loved. That part wasn't a lie. And as he slowly smiled at her she wished that the rest wasn't a lie. That she could be walking towards him to make vows that she would live the rest of her life by. How had she got herself into this mess? How could she have been naive enough to think that something like this could make things better and not worse?

It was a penance, that was what it was. By weaving a web of lies around the people that meant the most to her she had been in turn punished, by being shown something that she wanted more than she had ever even known.

But she of all people should have known that life was unfair.

The registrar took a step forward and started speaking the words that everyone expected to hear. Brendan then gave his daughter's hand into Aiden's and stepped back, moving into his place beside her mother at the head of the room.

Caitlin's eyes flickered to meet Aiden's, and then she looked over her shoulder at her family. She looked at each of their faces as they smiled at her, her mother dabbing at her eyes with a handkerchief. Would they understand? Would they forgive her?

Two sets of 'I do', and then the deed would be done.

Aiden's fingers squeezed around hers and she glanced down, frowning slightly at the chill she felt from his skin. She looked up at him, saw him avoid her eyes, watched his jaw clenching. And she felt cold right along her spine.

He released her hand as the man in front of them rhymed off his words, and Caitlin felt the distance between them as some giant void.

'Do you, Caitlin…?'

She tried to focus on the words, to say hers at the right time. And then the man looked at her, his eyes questioning. She swallowed to dampen her dry throat and managed a flat-toned, 'I do.'

She'd done her part.

Her eyes moved to Aiden as the words were repeated for him. He didn't turn to look at her. He frowned, he glanced upwards, and then he finally looked at her as the words finished.

A pin could have dropped in the room as he said nothing.

Caitlin stared at him. *I do.* She willed him to say the two words that would end the charade for them both. But he continued to stare at her with eyes that lacked their usual depth of warm blue.

She raised her brows in question.

He still stayed silent.

'What are you doing?' She whispered the words at him as he began to turn towards the sea of faces.

He took a breath and leaned slightly closer to her to whisper back, 'Remember your promise, Caitlin Rourke.'

What was he doing? He had to say 'I do' to complete the contract. And he hadn't said it!

'Aiden?'

Aiden shook his head and glanced at her from the corner of his eye. 'I'm sorry about this.'

Then he looked forward and took a step closer to the crowded room. He cleared his throat. 'Folks, I'm afraid there isn't going to be a wedding today.'

There were gasps in the crowd and a murmur of exclamations. Caitlin's father got to his feet.

Aiden held up a hand. 'If you'll just hear me out…'

Caitlin stepped towards him and grabbed his sleeve. 'What are you doing? You haven't said "I do". You're supposed to say it first.'

His eyes moved to hers again. 'That's just it, Caitlin. I was never going to say it.'

Her dark eyes widened in surprise. *What?* He'd never intended to complete this? He was stopping them both from getting the pay-off at the end? *Why?* Why would he put them through all this if he'd had no intention of it coming to its logical conclusion? *How* could he put her through this, be there to support her all this time, if he knew all along he had no intention of allowing her to do what she'd set out to do? It just didn't make any sense!

Her eyes strayed to her family, to her father's face. And she realised she'd failed. He would still lose the business he'd built from the ground; they would still lose the home they'd all grown up in. And her heart broke.

She removed her hand from Aiden's sleeve and stepped away from him as the tears formed in her eyes. She looked up at him, at the face of the man she'd thought she knew so well. *Who she'd trusted.* And it was like looking at a stranger.

He looked back at her family. 'Up until three months ago Caitlin and I had never met.'

Brendan frowned in confusion. 'Then what the hell is all this?'

'It's a TV Show. It's called *Fake Fiancé*.'

'It's *what*?' Her mother and brothers stood up and Brendan stepped towards Aiden, his hands clenching into fists at his sides. 'This is all some kind of joke?'

'No, sir. No joke,' Aiden took another breath and continued. 'Caitlin agreed to do this show, to fool all of you into thinking it was a real wedding...' he paused and added the final insult '...for money.'

Caitlin froze as a sob escaped her mother's throat, and she watched as disappointment entered her eyes. Then she looked at her father's face and saw the understanding. And then the anger. She started to shake uncontrollably.

'She believed that was why we were both doing this. That I was fooling all my friends the same way she was—for the same cash payment.' He turned slightly and looked at her. 'But that's not true.'

Tears streamed down her pale cheeks as she looked at him. 'What?'

Aiden's jaw clenched and unclenched. 'I was supposed to make things more difficult for you. It was my job to up the conflict by doing things like insisting on a big wedding when that was the last thing you wanted. That was the plan from the beginning.'

Caitlin shook her head slowly, suddenly making sense of that one occasion when he had done something she hadn't understood. But at the same time she was still confused.

Because if he'd been there to make things so difficult for her then why had he been so supportive? She would have quit long ago if he hadn't been there. Was that why he'd done it? To keep her in the show? Was there no end to the depth of his betrayal? Because that was what it was. *Betrayal.* Betrayal of her faith in him, of the depth of feelings she'd developed for him. For weeks now she'd been scared she would lose him. When in fact he'd never been there to begin with.

'*Why?*' The question forced itself from her mouth. What kind of person could do this to her?

'This is my show.' He waved a hand in the direction of Mick and Joe, who were moving in with the camera. 'These are my camera crews. I'm the producer of the show, Caitlin.'

The room went completely silent as she stared at him. Even her tears stopped. And the overwhelming emotion of love that she'd felt for him turned to hatred in a single heartbeat.

She turned away from him and looked at her family. She might have just lost one person that she cared about. But she had to try and salvage *something*. Her voice shook as she stepped towards her father. 'I had to try and get the money somehow.'

'By lying to us?' Brendan's face grew red as he held his emotions in check. 'You think it was worth all this?'

She watched as he waved his hand at the room.

'All these people came here for you. Because they care about you. And all the time you've been laughing behind their backs!'

'It wasn't like that!' She choked out the words as the tears came again. 'I hated lying to you all. It hurt every single day. But I had to try, Dad. I had to try to get the money.'

'Like this?' He shook his head and wrapped his arm around her mother, his eyes straying to the silent tears that streamed down her cheeks. Then he looked back at his daughter. 'Nothing is worth this, Caitlin. We could have lost everything else we had but we would always have had each other. I never thought you would be capable of this level of deceit.' He shook his head again. 'A family is worth far more than what's in its bank account. And now you've ruined any trust we ever had in you.'

A sob escaped Caitlin's throat as he turned and led her mother away from her, back down the aisle she'd just walked up. She then turned and looked at her bridesmaids as they walked past her.

Izzy just frowned and shook her head. But Cara, with tears in her eyes, stopped for a second in front of her.

'I knew something was wrong. You messed up big-style this time. How could you do this to us?'

They moved away from her and followed her parents.

Caitlin didn't see their path blocked by Aisling, because she turned towards Aiden. He'd been watching them leave too, a look of panic on his face. But as Caitlin stepped towards him he turned.

She slapped him hard across the face. 'I don't even need to tell you what you've done!'

She spat the words at him. 'Because you already know, don't you? *Whoever* you are.'

She stared at him for a long second, and then started down the aisle after the others. To say what when she got there, she didn't know. But she had to try.

'Caitlin, wait!'

She ignored the shouted words and picked up her skirts to walk faster.

'Stop them!' Aiden stepped down and walked towards her with long strides. 'I need you all to take a minute—*please!*'

Brendan turned around from where he'd been arguing with Aisling. 'Why in hell's name should we listen to anything else *you* have to say?'

Aiden stopped, stood a little taller, and raised his chin a visible inch. His words were determined. 'Because if you love your daughter even half as much as I know you do you'll want to understand why she did this.' His eyes strayed to Caitlin's back, where she stood frozen in the middle of the aisle. 'And how much it cost her every day doing it.'

When Brendan took a moment to consider his words, Aiden waded on in, his words softer. 'Mr Rourke, I think you know *why* she did it. Even if you don't know *how* she could do it. All I'm asking is that you take a few minutes so I can let you see what we've seen.'

The older man looked around at the faces of the rest of his family, and then into Caitlin's tormented eyes.

He folded his arms across his chest. 'You have five minutes, and then I fully expect never to have to hear your name again.'

CHAPTER TWENTY-ONE

AIDEN nodded, then turned and walked back up the steps at the front of the room. He turned to face the crowd again. 'When we first came up with the idea for this show we had a fairly firm idea of what we thought we'd get.'

Caitlin kept her back to him as his words sounded in the silent room.

'We live in a society that's now geared towards how successful a person is. Their worth is decided more on the amount in their bank account than on old-fashioned values like a solid family foundation and good friends. So we wanted to see how far someone would go to get what they wanted. Would they lie to the people they cared about to get richer? And how much of a fight would they put up if there was someone there to make it a more difficult journey for them? It was supposed to be all about the money.'

She closed her eyes. *Dear God.* Was that the kind of person everyone would think she was?

'But that's not what we got.' He took a breath and reached a hand up to loosen his tie and undo the top button of his shirt. 'It's not what we got. It's not what *I* saw. And what I saw every day with Caitlin didn't just change the show, it changed me.'

Her eyes opened.

'What we got made a complete lie out of all the premises we started with. Because this wasn't about some mercenary woman who was prepared to use her family and friends to get a big pay-off.' He spoke to her back. 'Which, incidentally, you've still got. Even though I didn't say the ''I do''. That was never in question.'

She didn't even care about that any more. The chances of her now persuading her father to take it were slim to none at all. It had all been a waste of time. But she stayed silent and listened.

'I guess we picked the wrong family to show that there weren't family values any more. The show we've been filming these last few months isn't about the lack of family values now, it's about the very real existence of them. When people see what we've seen they'll realise that having a family as close as the Rourkes is still possible. It still matters. It still stands for something.'

Brendan finally looked at Caitlin. And something in his eyes seemed to soften. She stared back at her father through her tears.

'Caitlin didn't do this for herself.' Aiden smiled slightly. 'A wise man told me recently that loving someone means giving before you take anything for yourself. And that's what Caitlin was doing—trying to give something back to the people she loves.'

Aiden felt his throat thicken. He glanced across at Aisling, who smiled at him in encouragement. So he cleared his throat again. 'The show is now about love. In all its forms. The love of a family, the love of friends. And what one person is prepared to risk to fight for those things.'

Brendan slowly smiled at Caitlin, his eyes sparkling. Almost imperceptibly his head nodded. And Caitlin sobbed again when she realised he understood.

'When I decided to play the fiancé in this, rather than getting someone else, I did it because I thought it would give me a chance to direct things in the way I thought they should go. I guess I'm a bit of a control freak that way.' He smiled wryly. 'But the truth is that as soon as I got to know Caitlin everything was taken out of my hands.'

Caitlin blinked slowly and gradually turned around.

'I didn't lie about anything apart from my involvement in the show and what I do for a living.' He finally got to look into her eyes, and for a second words failed him.

'And that makes what you did okay?' Izzy spoke the words that Caitlin couldn't.

'No, it doesn't.' He shook his head. 'But I had to finish what I'd started or Caitlin wouldn't get the money.'

'What a hero.'

'Oh, don't worry. I'm paying for it, Izzy.' He ran his fingers back through his hair. 'Because somewhere along the way the laugh was on me.'

Caitlin stared as he looked back at her.

'You see, the fact is I fell in love. And that wasn't supposed to happen.'

All eyes in the room moved from Aiden to Caitlin, where she stood frozen to the spot. She could feel them looking, could sense the anticipation. And while they looked she stared into Aiden's blue, blue eyes. Then she shook her head.

'Nice try.'

Aiden watched as she turned away and walked into her father's embrace. The entire family then turned together and moved towards the double doors at the end of the room.

He raised his voice. 'There didn't seem to be any other way of explaining to everyone here what has happened this last few months. So the best way to make everything clear is to just show you.'

Aisling took a step back and flicked off the lights, and at the top of the room one of Aiden's team uncovered a large screen.

Then in the darkness titles played, and the rich timbre of a voice-over sounded in the silence.

'Is there love in the world any more? We all like to hope so. It's the one thing that binds us together—the invisible force that makes people do things they never knew they were capable of. And, no matter how we may fool ourselves into believing we can live without it, the simple truth is no one can…'

Her mother turned around first, then Cara, until one by one all the people who mattered to Caitlin were looking at the screen.

'Caitlin Rourke could be any one of us. She has a family and friends. She has a career she's worked hard to be successful at. She's loved and lost along the way…'

Izzy watched pictures of Caitlin flicker across the screen, then looked at her in the darkness and whispered, 'Take a look, sweetie.'

Caitlin shook her head.

'*But she took the biggest gamble of her life to give something special to her family. To do that she had to tell the biggest lie she'd ever told, and fool them all into believing it…*'

She heard Aiden's low voice echo around the room from the screen.

'*So how do we make them all believe we're in love, Caitlin Rourke?*'

'*She had to make everyone believe she was getting married when she wasn't. Her fake fiancé was Aiden Flynn and he was going to show us all that people are capable of anything for money. Instead he found out that people are capable of anything for love…*'

The voice faded away and was replaced by the haunting sound of Irish Uilleann pipes, violins, and an acoustic guitar. And Caitlin finally turned around to look at the images on the screen.

She saw her own face as she asked him, '*Aiden Flynn, are you flirting with me?*'

'*Is it working?*'

She saw herself lean in closer to whisper, *'No.'*

Then there were images of them together: talking, arguing, smiling. Then there was their first kiss in the garden. The music continued to play softly in the background, the pipes haunting as a love story played across the screen.

Caitlin's mother's voice then. *'I'm so glad you found him, you know. It's what I've wanted for you for such a long time now.'*

More images showed Caitlin crying as the tangled web started to close in on her. The anguish written on her face in close-up detail.

Then Aiden's whispered voice. *'...it won't be hard to convince everyone that I'm crazy about you, Caitlin Rourke. You see, I already am.'*

Caitlin felt heavy tears drop slowly off the ends of her lashes while the crowded room watched what they had lived through.

She was with Mike in the garden. Mike's voice was sounding over the music. *'...he never looked at any of them the way he looks at you.'*

'And what way does he look at me?'

'Like you're the most important thing in his life. Some kind of precious gift he has to take care of. There's nothing fake about the attachment he has to you. I don't think anyone would think there was.'

Caitlin's eyes strayed from the images on the screen to Aiden. He was standing back from the screen, his face hidden in shadows.

The music swelled as his voice sounded again. *'Do you regret doing this, Caitlin Rourke?'*

'I don't regret meeting you. I won't ever forget that.'

'And I won't ever regret knowing you. You have to know that.'

'I do know. I just wish sometimes that we'd met some other way.'

'Me too.'

He stepped forward from the shadows and looked at her. and Caitlin's heart caught at the look on his face. He loved her. If the images on the screen didn't show her that then the telltale shimmer in his eyes surely should.

He blinked hard and looked up at the screen as the voice-over returned. 'Fake Fiancé. *It's about the love that's still possible for all of us. The love of family, the love of friends. And love when it's least expected...'*

Her own voice sounded against a background of acoustic guitar. *'I'm scared I'll lose you.'*

'You'll never lose me, honey. I'll always be here, for as long as you want me to be. It's always your choice. I want you to remember that. Promise me.'

There was a side shot as he tried to leave, and then came back to kiss her as if his life depended on it.

Her voice sounded again. *'I promise.'*

And as the lights came back on Caitlin remembered what he'd said before the truth had come out. *'Remember your promise, Caitlin Rourke.'*

Her heart pounding, she looked up at his bowed head. His shoulders were slumped slightly, as if all the fight had left him. But he'd just fought harder for her than anyone ever had. He'd taken a chance—a big one. He had stood at the front of a room full of people and told the truth, hadn't he? She wanted so badly to believe it. But could she?

Caitlin lifted her chin, ignoring the eyes on her as she walked up the aisle to him. He didn't look up until she was a step away.

'Why should I believe you after all this, Aiden?' Her eyes flickered slightly as a thought crossed her mind. 'If that's even what your name is.'

'It is. And I can't think of any reason you should trust me right now.' He looked down for a second, and then back into her eyes. 'Except that it's the truth, Caitlin. I *am* the person you've spent all this time with. I just do something different for a living.'

'Making tacky TV shows that pull families apart?'

He grimaced. 'Okay, I deserved that. But not everything I do is like this show.'

Caitlin raised a disbelieving brow.

'These things just happen to be popular at the minute.' He cleared his throat, his voice dropping. 'And they wanted a ratings-winner from me before they'd let me film something more important to me. So I agreed.'

The penny dropped and her eyes widened. 'Your book?'

'Yes.' He stepped closer, his low words meant only for her ears. 'I didn't lie about anything else. I promise you that. And when you told me why you were really doing this I couldn't quit. Not because of the deal I'd made, but because I wanted to see it through for *you*. Even if it meant I'd lose you.'

She shrugged her shoulders, maintaining a cool exterior even as his words reached out to her. 'You could have tried just telling me.'

'I wanted to.'

'But you wanted your father's work shown more?'

'I'm not going to lie and tell you I wouldn't still have tried to find a way to get it done. I have to, so I can close the door on that part of my life and move on. But I'd have given up on it rather than see you hurt the way you were.' He had to stop and clear his throat again. 'But you needed this thing done, so I had to take a chance.'

Caitlin stared into his eyes for a long, long moment. She wanted so badly to believe him. To believe in what she'd seen on the screen.

'How do I know this isn't all just part of the show now? That you didn't plan from the start to get me to fall for you?'

Aiden frowned at her reasoning. 'You think I'm that sure of myself? Caitlin, I'm still not that sure of what you feel. If I knew I wouldn't be standing here right now, laying my heart on the line in front of a room full of people.'

She watched as he ran his fingers through his hair, then waved his arm to the side, 'Do you want me to drop all this? To cancel the programme? Because if that's what it takes to show you then I'll do it.'

A small burst of sarcastic laughter escaped her mouth, some of her pain seeping out. 'Oh, sure. You're going to do that after all this hard work you've put into it?'

His shoulders slumped again as he realised he had lost. He wasn't going to convince her. No matter what he said. Taking a breath, he blinked back his emotion and forced himself to speak in a steady voice. 'What you saw on that screen was the truth, Caitlin. I didn't know any other way of showing you. And if airing it the way it is now has some other cynic like me believing in love, then at least something good will come out of it.'

Caitlin watched as he turned away from her and took two steps up the carpeted stairs. Then he stopped, and she saw his shoulders rise as he took a breath before he turned and stepped back to her.

'I love you. I love you more than I thought I was capable of loving anyone. And even if I had to steal that time from you, Caitlin Rourke, you can't take it back from me. Because for a few months I got to know what it was like to be a whole person. And for that I'm going to thank you. Even if I can't convince you it's true.' He smiled sadly. 'Like I just said on that screen, I wish we'd met some other way.'

She watched with blinking eyes as he looked back at her father. 'She's paid a high price for all this, Mr Rourke. I hope you'll respect the fact that she did it all out of love and for no other reason. Don't punish her for that by not accepting what she's worked so hard for.'

And she heard her father's voice, strained with emotion as he answered. 'I won't, son.'

She watched again as Aiden looked back at her, then turned away for a second time. To leave. Because there wasn't really anything else he could say to her, was there? He'd taken a shot at convincing her, had laid everything on the line for her. Had offered to dump the show that would in turn lead to the dumping of the project the Aiden she'd known cared so much about. And he had even tried to fix things for her with her father before he walked away.

Her heart decided for her. Because even though it had just suffered the worst kind of knock it had had since Liam had died, the tearing of it inside her chest at the thought of him leaving her for ever was more than she could take. So she followed her heart.

'I believe you.'

He froze at the softly spoken words.

'I shouldn't. But I do.'

He slowly turned around.

'I guess the thing about love is that occasionally you have to take a chance on it.'

He moved back towards her.

'But I truly hated you for a while there.'

He nodded. 'I knew you would.'

She made the final step to him, then lifted her chin to look into his ridiculously blue eyes. 'And yet you still took a chance on making this work. That's what the Aiden I knew would have done.' She smiled. 'You really do love me, Aiden Flynn?'

Aiden smiled back, his heart in his eyes. 'Yes, Caitlin Rourke. I do.'

She smiled again at the irony of him saying the two words she'd expected him to say much earlier on. Her head tilted to one side and she reached for his hand. 'I love you too. I have for a long time now. You'll just need to spend the rest of your life convincing me that what we feel was never a lie.'

He took her hand in his. 'I will.'

A pair of hands started clapping behind them, and they turned to watch as Brendan led the applause. He nodded at Aiden as the rest of the room joined in.

'I have an idea!' Aiden leaned down to shout in her ear. Then he dragged her off to one side as the room filled with the sound of voices talking about the proceedings. 'Marry me. That way I'll never have to take a chance on losing you again.'

Caitlin's eyes widened and she laughed. 'We can't get married, you idiot.' She pointed her finger behind her. 'That's an actor up there—remember?'

'I remember. But Father Mike is a real priest.'

Her laughter died and she gaped at him. 'But this isn't real.'

'Honey, this is very real. And so is our marriage registration'

Caitlin stood in stunned silence as his words sank in. She stared up at him and saw the light in his eyes. She believed that everything she'd thought was real about him was. He'd said the only things he hadn't told her were about his involvement in the show and what he did for a living. And, looking at the hope on his face, she knew he hadn't lied to her about anything else. How he'd been with her, how he'd felt, had always been real. Just as how she'd been with him and how she'd felt. He loved her. She loved him. Did it really matter how they'd got to here?

He leaned his head towards hers. 'Marry me and I promise you that every day I'll make up for the pain I caused us both.'

She reached her fingers up into the hair at the nape of his neck and pulled his mouth to hers. 'You'd better say ''I do'' this time.'

Aiden smiled. 'I will. I'm never letting you go.'

Marrying him after all the lies and deceit might not make much sense. But to Caitlin it was the most truly honest thing she could ever do.

Because Aiden was right about the new format for his show. It really was all about love. What else was there?

MILLS & BOON® PUBLISH EIGHT LARGE PRINT TITLES A MONTH. THESE ARE THE EIGHT TITLES FOR MAY 2006

❧

THE SHEIKH'S INNOCENT BRIDE
Lynne Graham

BOUGHT BY THE GREEK TYCOON
Jacqueline Baird

THE COUNT'S BLACKMAIL BARGAIN
Sara Craven

THE ITALIAN MILLIONAIRE'S VIRGIN WIFE
Diana Hamilton

HER ITALIAN BOSS'S AGENDA
Lucy Gordon

A BRIDE WORTH WAITING FOR
Caroline Anderson

A FATHER IN THE MAKING
Ally Blake

THE WEDDING SURPRISE
Trish Wylie

MILLS & BOON®

Live the emotion

0406 Rom LP

MILLS & BOON® PUBLISH EIGHT LARGE PRINT TITLES A MONTH. THESE ARE THE EIGHT TITLES FOR JUNE 2006

———————— ❦ ————————

THE HIGH-SOCIETY WIFE
Helen Bianchin

THE VIRGIN'S SEDUCTION
Anne Mather

TRADED TO THE SHEIKH
Emma Darcy

THE ITALIAN'S PREGNANT MISTRESS
Cathy Williams

FATHER BY CHOICE
Rebecca Winters

PRINCESS OF CONVENIENCE
Marion Lennox

A HUSBAND TO BELONG TO
Susan Fox

HAVING THE BOSS'S BABIES
Barbara Hannay

MILLS & BOON®

Live the emotion

0506 Ror